Subject: Why You Love My Coolio E-Mails
From: Mrs.Oded@btelecom.co.uk
To: Dru@seattlegrrl.com

1. I tell you everything about my hunkalicious boyfriend, right down to the kissing, and I just bet no one else tells you about what it feels like to kiss a hottalicious guy with an über-fabu mustache.
2. My firm grasp on the very latest English slang, words like "chuff" (say it wrong and it could mean fart) and "fwoar" (I have no idea what it means, but it sounds very cool, don't you think?).
3. I have naturally good taste, so you can trust me when I tell you just how pervo the skirts they make us wear for field hockey are—and we're talking majorly pervo, here.
4. Did I mention kissing a hottie with a mustache?
5. You feel much better about your family because you don't have a father called Brother, a mother who is keen to give you sex talks, or a sister who tries to drag you to every weirdo radical protest she can find.
6. Who else do you know who lives in a creepy house and sleeps in a tower room with its own ghost?
7. Detailed, in-depth analyses, biographies, and descriptions of snogworthy English guys who are on my Potential Boyfriend List.
8. My insightful and totally fabulous advice on your own love life. (Get over Vance the Weasel, babe!)
9. KISSING, KISSING, KISSING! 'Nuff said, right? Right. I knew that would convince you.

Hugs and kisses,
~Em

S0-ASF-268

THE Year
My Life
WENT DOWN
THE Loo

Katie Maxwell

smooch

New York City

SMOOCH®

September 2003

Published by

Dorchester Publishing Co., Inc.
276 Fifth Avenue
New York, NY 10001

The name "SMOOCH" and its logo are trademarks of Dorchester Publishing Co., Inc.

Printed in the United States of America.

Visit us on the web at www.smoochya.com.

There are always so many people I want to thank for helping me when I write a book, and this one is no exception. I fawn upon the feet of Kate Seaver, editor extraordinaire and the brain behind the SMOOCH line, and likewise worship Michelle Grajkowski, my wonder-agent who always laughs at my jokes (no matter how bad they are). I also owe hugs and big smoochy kisses to Vance Briceland (who makes me look forward to sending him chunks of the book for critiquing, not to mention letting me take his name in vain), and my husband for putting up with me locking myself away in the computer room for days on end. A final thank you goes to actor Oded Fehr for being so dishy that he makes Emily swoon.

The Year My Life Went Down The Loo

Subject: I'm here safely in hell, thank you
From: Mrs.Oded@btelecom.co.uk
To: Dru@seattlegrrl.com
Date: 2 September 2003 6:13 pm

GAH! My room is haunted! And not just haunted by any old run-of-the-mill ghost—oh, no, my ghost is an underwear pervert!

Dru, Dru, dear, sweet Dru, I can't begin to tell you just how awful my life is. Well, OK, I can, and since I'm having to suffer, you, as my *numero uno* best friend, are going to have to suffer with me. Even though you're halfway around the world from me, you'll still suffer with me, won't you? 'Cause I'd do it for you. You know I would. I always get sympathy cramps for you, don't I?

Where should I start in the catalog of horror that is now my life? Well, first of all, don't be surprised if you get a letter from Brother or my mom saying I died (my obituary will read: *Emily Williams, sixteen but looks eighteen, died Tuesday night of a broken heart after being torn from her friends and home in a mondo cool area of Seattle—conveniently located to both malls and water parks—and dragged all the way to England, a country that STILL HAS DISCOS!*). This place is . . . well, I don't want to say it's awful, because there're castles and cool stuff like that, and the guys sound really sexy with their English accents, but gah! Everything is so friggin' old! It's "Oh, look at that, Emily, that building is five hundred years old" this, and, "That piece of Stonehenge has been standing in that spot for fifty gazillion years" that.

Well, duh! It's a rock! It's not like it's going to sprout legs, buy a thong, and go to Tahiti for a windsurfing vacation, now, is it?

That was Brother who said the bit about the rock, BTW (the first bit, not the thong part). You know him— the man lives for old stuff like that. Needless to say he's in seventh heaven here in Ye Olde Englande. So, anyway, I survived the move. Little tip from me to you: if your parents suggest moving you away from your rightful home to live in another country for a year, making you give up everything that's important, do not, under any circumstances, agree to go sightseeing with them. Especially if your dad is a medieval scholar like Brother, 'cause I'm here to tell you that you'll end up looking at nothing but stupid old rocks and buildings that should be plowed under to make room for more malls. You wouldn't believe this, but I've been here two whole days, and all we've seen are libraries!

"Can't we go see Windsor Castle?" I asked, thinking that Prince William guy might be hanging around there.

"Maybe another day. Brother wants to see a very old illuminated manuscript," Mom said. "It's very important to his research to see it in person."

"How about the dungeon museum? I heard there's one in London. That's not only very cool, it's historical, too. Bet there's medieval stuff there."

"Another time, Em," Brother said, and went off about how wonderful the library was that we were going to. I tell you, Dru, I was going crazy being trapped in the car with them, traveling from library to library having to look at a bunch of moldy old books.

Anyhoodles, I survived the sightseeing (if I ever see another illuminated manuscript, I may just ralph), and Brother's driving on the wrong side of everything, and yesterday we arrived here at Chez Williams aka the Haunted Mansion.

"What's wrong, Brother?" I asked when he pulled up before a creepy, old, creepy, dirty, and did I say creepy? house that looked like it should have been condemned. "Are we lost? Out of gas? Did the engine fall out?"

"Nope," that horrible man who spawned me answered in a cheerful *I can't wait to see this antiquity* sort of way that for the last two days had made the flesh on my back crawl. "This is our home away from home for the next year. Isn't it charming?"

Charming? The Amityville Horror looked more welcoming than the monstrosity that slouched at the end of the drive. Honest to Pete, Dru, it positively *reeked* of old!

"I am *so* not doing this," I said, taking a stand.

"It certainly is different than anything we have at home," Mom said, ignoring my stand-taking in that mom sort of way older women have. (The score so far—Emily: 0, Parental Units: 2.) "When did Professor Carlston say it was built?"

"In 1588, by Dracula, no doubt," I answered, gripping my purse firmly. If anything creepy even thought about grabbing me, I'd nail it upside the head with twenty-two pounds of makeup.

"Now, Emily, you know that Vlad the Impaler was born in 1421. It would have been impossible for him to build this house in 1588," Brother said. "Ten points if you can tell me during what empire Vlad ruled Wallacia."

I am warning you right here and now, Dru—if your father gives you even the slightest reason to think he'll ever become a scholar, kill him. I know that seems harsh, but honestly, the historical pop quizzes alone are grounds for divorcing him as a parent. "Can we skip the pop quizzes and get right down to the exorcism?" I asked as The Parents hustled me toward the house. It's huge, I mean really huge, and old, and black and moldy-looking, with all sorts of windows that poke out and glare down on you. "Do either of you have any holy water?"

"It certainly does have atmosphere," Mom said.

"How about a spare crucifix or two?"

"Emily . . . " Brother said warningly. He did something to the front door and it squeaked open. Inside was a whole lot of black. I swear you could hear the bats rubbing their little batty paws together and cackling at the fresh dinner walking in.

"A Bible? A *What Would Jesus Do* sticker?"

"Not now, Em," Mom said, pulling me in to the abyss. The door slammed shut behind us.

"Abandon hope, all ye who enter here."

Brother eyed me. "She didn't get that smart mouth from *my* side of the family."

Mom smiled and patted him on the arm. "It's a defense mechanism, dear. Girls Emily's age feel it's vital to appear flip on the outside even though they're riddled with insecurities on the inside."

Gah! Mothers!!!

"Are you sure she's mine?" Brother asked Mom in what passes for Old-People humor. "Is it too late for a paternity test?"

I'll save you from the horrors of the grand tour, as the Sperm Donor called it. Let me just say that the house is one big creepfest. If there aren't hockey-mask-wearing, homicidal, deranged ax murderers living in the basement, you can paint my toenails and call me Sally. And you know I *hate* the name Sally.

Must go. Brother just bellowed upstairs that dinner is on, and it'll probably take me at least a week to find my way down to the ground floor (that's first floor to you and the rest of the world). I'll tell you about the underwear ghost later. Oh, yeah, note my English e-mail addy. Oh! Oh! Oh! I picked up a magazine at the airport that said Oded was in England filming a new movie—can you believe that Brother had no idea who he was?

"He's only the star of *The Mummy* and *The Mummy Returns*, two of the hottest movies ever made in the whole history of the universe!" I told him, then made him look at my Oded scrapbooks (the one with the pictures from both Mummy movies, not the ones with the pictures of Oded on the TV shows). Brother pretended to stagger away after he sat through the three Mummy scrapbooks, which was just so funny I forgot to laugh. Sheesh! He makes me look at old books for two whole days, then squawks about a little Oded-viewing?

Oh, get this, you're going to die—the studio that Oded will be working at is only ten miles away! Eat your heart out, you poor Oded-less thing, you. Bet I marry him before you do!

Hugs and kisses,
~Em

P.S. How's the leg? What happened to your Sim Zombie family? Did Morticia Zombie marry Ted Townie? YOU HAVE TO TELL ME!!!

Subject: Re: the panty ghost
From: Mrs.Oded@btelecom.co.uk
To: Dru@seattlegrrl.com
Date: 2 September 2003 11:44 pm

Dru wrote:
> *What do you mean, you have a ghost in your room?*
> *You just can't say something like that and then tell*
> *me you have to go down to dinner! What if I never*
> *hear from you again? What if the ghost gets you?*
> *Who will have sympathy cramps for me then?*

Calm down, panicked one. I'm OK. The ghost doesn't seem to be interested in anything but my undies. Which is creepy enough, let me tell you! The thought of spectral hands fondling my bras gives me the willies.

Here's what happened—we arrived two days ago. Since Bess was allowed—unfairly (what makes it all right for her to get to do things just because she's eighteen?)—to tour England by herself for a whole week, I got the first dibs on the best bedroom. Brother and Mom took the Old People's room downstairs (so the Ancient One doesn't have to climb the stairs every night, and let me tell you, that's a blessing for those of us who like to sleep at night. Brother's knees sound like cannons going off when he climbs stairs. I'm working on Mom to get him a StairMaster for Christmas, heh heh heh). So there I was with pick of the prime rooms, and of course, having exceptional taste, I chose the tower room. Now get this—the room is almost totally round! There's a turret or spire or whatever they call it overhead, but the room itself is round, with great window seats. Of course, the first thing I did was check the storage space under the window seats for dead bodies, severed limbs, pulsating hearts, etc., but they were empty.

Fine and dandy, say I, and I snaffle the room. Since appearance is everything, I unpacked right away and got my clothes put away in this big old piece of furni-

ture Brother says is a wardrobe (don't the English understand the necessity of a really big walk-in closet?), and
tuck the undies and stuff away in a dresser. A side note:
I can't *believe* Mom only let me bring two suitcases.
How can I go out in public with only two suitcases full
of clothes? I'm going shopping just as soon as I find out
where the nearest mall is.

Anyway, I go off and do family stuff and when I come
back, my underwear is ALL OVER THE ROOM! It was
soooo creepy! I, of course, did the only thing I could do.
I screamed.

Brother cracked and popped his way up the stairs
(which was really kind of nice of him considering how
old he is), and charged into the room looking like a fifty-
two-year-old deranged rhinoceros—he had a hair thing
going on that looked just like a horn. I really need to
have a talk with him about the benefits of mousse.

"What's wrong? Are you hurt? What happened?" he
asked in between gasps for air.

I stared pointedly at my undies lying all over the floor.
"My underwear is all over the room!"

He looked around, the hair horn kind of quivering in
an agitated sort of way. "Your underwear?"

There are times when I am *positive* that he doesn't
speak the same language I do. "Underwear. As in, those
things I wear under my clothes? Get it? Underwear?"

"I know what underwear is, Emily. And I can do without that smart tone."

Oh, right, this from the man who springs Vlad the
Impaler trivia quizzes at the drop of a hat. "What*ever*."

He ruffled back the horn o' hair and looked around
the room again. "Why have you strewn your clothes
around the room? I thought you were excited about

having the tower room?"

"I didn't strew anything around, Old One. I put my things—pitiful and in need of immediate replacement—in the drawer, but when I got back, they were all over the floor. I just *knew* this house was haunted, and now I've got proof." I shook an underwire bra at him. "We've got ghosts. I just hope you're happy! God only knows what the ghost is going to do with my—"

Oops! Almost let the cat out of the bag there. Don't want him to find out about my erotic-massage kit.

"With your what?" Brother asked.

"My . . . um . . . " I had to think fast. You know how suspicious my father can be. "Um . . . my personal things. You know, women's things."

"Oh." He didn't look like he believed me. "Regardless of that, there are no such things as ghosts, Emily. You probably simply forgot to put your things away."

"Fwah! Even if I did forget—and I didn't, because unlike some members of this family who are so ancient they can recall what the Holy Grail looks like, I can remember things—but even if I did forget, I would not have thrown all my underwear around the room. Thus, therefore, and all that other stuff, either there's an ax-murdering maniac with an underwear fetish living in the basement who came up here while I was hooking up the computer downstairs, or this room is haunted."

"Emily—"

"I'd prefer a ghost to an ax murderer, thank you."

"You can always use another room if you don't like this one."

"But I do like it," I said, grabbing the rest of my things and stuffing them back into the drawer. "It's the only cool room in this whole nightmare of a house. You always say I have to make the best of a bad situation, and in this case, that means I get the cool room. It's only fair."

"Fine," he said, running his hand through his hair again. It only made the horn stand up even more. "If you're done having this morning's histrionics, I have work to do. The dean of the college I'll be working for is coming by in a few minutes. I trust you'll be available to greet him?"

What is it with parents having you meet all their cronies? All they do is criticize your hair and ask you what you want to do when you grow up. Hello! I'm grown up. But never let it be said that I, Emily Williams, let an opportunity slip past me. "Let's make a deal," I said.

Brother groaned. "Not now, Emily—"

"The deal is this: I come down and be charming and pleasant to your dean, and you take me to the nearest mall."

"I don't have time to drive you around. I've got to be ready for the start of term next week—and speaking of that, so do you. Don't you want to bone up before you start school?"

I shuddered. Well, you know my feelings about that whole school thing—it's going to be even more of a hell than my life already is. I don't know anyone in England! I don't even know what they study here! What if they think I'm weird because I'm American? GAH! I figured I'd better change the subject. "About the mall—"

"Not today, sweetling," he said as he creaked and popped his way out of the room. I rolled my eyes at the "sweetling." He uses those medieval words on purpose. He thinks they're cute. Fathers! "Maybe your mother can take you. I'll expect you downstairs in fifteen minutes."

"I can't."

"Why?" he asked, pausing at the door.

I waved my hand at the wardrobe. "I don't have anything to wear. That's why I have to go to the mall."

"What you have on is fine. Downstairs in fifteen, missy, and none of your sulks, please."

I hate it when the parents pull that authority crap on me. Sulks—*excuse* me, I'm sixteen! I don't sulk! I have never sulked! I don't even know how to sulk!

I thought about ignoring the order altogether, but figured it might peeve off Mom if I did, which would lessen the chance of getting her to drive me to the nearest mall. Besides, it wasn't like this dean person was anyone important. It didn't matter what I wore. Right?

A few minutes later, there I was, the picture of everything fabulous, sitting in the room Brother calls the library, but which really looks (and smells) like a mouse's playroom—it's full of a bunch of boring old books, not even the good kind like that Victorian erotica book I found (you remember, the one with all the "manly pillars of alabaster"). This stuff is sermons and other deadly things like that—and Brother brings in this old guy who's the head of the college or something. I start to stand up to shake his hand, when this totally fabulous hottie comes in behind the dean. Girl, I'm telling you, I must have swallowed back *gallons* of slobber!

So I'm standing there and Brother does the introduction thing, and I find out that this hottie is named Aidan, and he's the dean's son, and I'm thinking that this is it, I've met the perfect man. He's all blond and hunkalicious and has dark gray eyes, and I swear to you, he's got a mustache! A MUSTACHE!

Oh, poop, I have to go. Mom insists I go with her to the grocery store, and since we made a deal (more about that later), I have to go. I'll e-mail you as soon as I'm back. You need to hear about Aidan and why I almost committed Brother-acide.

Hugs and kisses,
~Em

Subject: Re: AIDAN? YOU MET A GUY NAMED AIDAN????
From: Mrs.Oded@btelecom.co.uk
To: Dru@seattlegrrl.com
Date: 3 September 2003 6:02 pm

> *EMILY MARIE WILLIAMS! You can't just tell me you*
> *met a hottie with a mustache and then leave me*
> *hanging! Tell me everything! Every single thing!*

Hold on there, GF, I said I'd e-mail you as soon as I got back. We had to go to some bass-ackwards grocery store that was filled with foreign food (stuff you can't even imagine people eating—mushy peas? What's up with that? Who wants their peas mushy?). Then we got lost coming home, which was kind of fun b/c Mom likes to check out the same sorts of stuff I do (anything that's *not* a library), and after that Brother made me go with them to some stupid party at Oxford. Or rather, one of the colleges. I know, it's confusing, I thought Oxford *was* a college, but it's like a mega college, and there's all these little colleges within it. I think. I wasn't really paying attention when Brother was going on and on and on about it on the way to Oxford.

Aidan of the mustache wasn't at the party, which was major dullsville, let me tell you. Imagine a room full of zombies sipping politely at their drinkies and talking about politics and other boring stuff. Anyway, on the way home, I noticed this sign on the side of the road that said *Piddlington-on-the-Weld 1km*. I was just starting to snicker to myself about all the poor people that live in Piddling-on-the-wheel when Brother pulled off at the POTW exit.

"Hey," I said. You know me, never one to pull my punches. "What are you doing? Taking a shortcut to Ghoul Central? How come we've turned off here?"

"We live here, Emily."

Honest to Pete, I just about piddled on the weld (whatever that is). "*WHAT?* You said we live in a town called Alling! No one ever said anything about a town that describes someone peeing on something!"

Brother glared at me in the rearview mirror. "Piddlington is a suburb of Alling. The town name has nothing to do with urine. Many British towns bear old and ancient names dating back . . . "

I groaned to myself and tried to stop listening. Whenever Brother gets going on anything ancient, he can talk until the end of time. I can't believe they made me move to a town called Piddlington! As if things weren't horrible enough, now I am forever going to be cursed as being known as "Emily, that girl from Piddlesville." Let's take a closer look at just exactly how my life has turned into a hellish nightmare, K?

- I am forced to leave BFF Dru and other friends for a whole year.
- I have to go to a new school with new kids in a new country.

- Things are different here! I stand out because of my accent (not that I have one, but everyone here thinks I do).
- I'm missing a whole year of AP physics. I won't be able to take my SATs until next fall. How can I get into a good college without having taken AP classes and the SATs?
- I had to give up my job at the music store, which means not only will I now have to live on just my allowance (miniscule), but I won't get free CDs and stuff anymore.
- I don't know anyone here but Mom and Brother and Bess!
- Here = Weewee-on-the-weld.
- I was going to have Mr. Benson for both AP physics and calculus this year, and you know how fun his classes are! He's the only teacher I like and now I won't have him at all!

Back to Aidan and what happened yesterday. So, we're standing in the library, and Brother and the dean are talking about something (probably ancient brass stuff or medieval tortures or those horribly dull books he insists on dragging us to see), and I'm being very cool about Aidan. I didn't drool on him or throw myself on him or anything even remotely like asking him if he'd like to go up to my room and get busy.

"So you're going to Gob-botty?" he asked with an insouciant smile. (What's insouciant? It was on today's "Words So Obscure You'll Never Use Them" calendar. Go look it up. I'll wait.)

"Gob-botty? I thought it was Gobottle School."

He grinned. My knees melted. I had to hold on to the

chair to keep up the pretense that I was standing.

"Everyone calls it Gob-botty. *Botty*, you know?"

"Oh, of course," I laughed with him. "Botty. Hahahahahahah." What the heck is a botty? What is with these people and their obscure jokes? GAH!

(An FYI . . . I just did an Internet search. Seems "botty" is slang for "butt." Oh, great. My new school's name means butt-mouth. Lovely. In Piddle City. Can I die now, please?)

"I'm in the sixth form. I'll do two years of study, then I'll be going to Magdalen."

"Magdalen!" I said, brightly and with much coolness and not at all like I hadn't the slightest idea who or what Magdalen was, which you know I didn't, but as I said, appearance is everything when you're trying to convince someone you're fabu. "That's totally rufous! What are you . . . um . . . going to do there?"

"Law," he said. "Dad is a Magdalen man. Rufous? Doesn't that mean red?"

"Yeah, red, you know, as in, coolio? Kind of like green, but much better."

"Coolio?" He tipped his adorable little head to the side and scrunched up his gorgeous gray eyes.

"Cool is cool, but very cool is coolio."

He grinned. "I like the way you talk."

He likes the way I talk! He *likes* the way I talk! Maybe it won't be so bad here after all!

"Yeah, well, I do come from Seattle. We're very tight out there. So if you're going to Gob-Bottom, too, that means we might . . . um . . . you know, see each other. In classes and stuff."

He batted his lashes over his big, gray eyes and smiled at me. SMILED! A hottie with a mustache smiled at me! Do you think it's too early to sign up at the bridal registry?

"I'm sure we will. You're in the sixth form then, too?"

"I think so. Brother said something about the school. I'm sixteen, so that sounds about right."

"Brother?"

"My father. Everyone calls him Brother, even my mom and my grandma. He hates his real name. We humor him."

He nodded. "Sounds like you will be in the sixth form, too. Maybe I could show you around the school before term begins."

Are you insanely jealous with my femme fatale-ness yet? You should be! I only met Aidan (and how cool is that name? AIDAN! Aidan and Emily . . . has a nice ring to it, doesn't it?) for a few minutes and already he was asking me out on a date!

"I'm sure Emily would like that," Brother said, nosing into *my* conversation as if he had a right to. He had his boring old dean to talk to. Who told him he could snag my hottie, too? "She's been a bit nervous about starting school in a country well known for its academic excellence."

Brother told Aidan the mega hottie that *I* was nervous? Death, take me now!

"I'm sure she'll have no difficulties whatsoever," the dean guy said, giving me one of those old-people smiles (you know, the kind where their dry old lips peel back to expose dentures. Uck!). "Going into the sixth form, too, are you, young lady?"

I opened my mouth to say yes, but Brother slapped a big old hammy hand down on my shoulder and hauled me up to his side. Honest to Pete, Dru, I just about died of embarrassment . . . until he totally and completely ruined my life with what he said next.

"Fifth form, actually, dean, old bean." Or something like that. Brother is taking this living in England thing way too seriously. "Her mother and I thought she wouldn't be ready for the GSCE yet, and the headmaster at Gobottle agreed."

"What's the fifth form?" I asked, digging my elbow into his side so he'd let go of me. "What's a GSCE?"

"Fifth form?" Aidan asked, stroking a finger over his 'stache. It was such a very cool move, I almost piddled . . . I mean, *puddled* up right there. "But she's sixteen. She should be in the sixth form, not the fifth. The fifth formers are younger."

A horrible, awful, ghastly, *terrible* thought occurred to me then. I turned on Brother and tried to sound like I wasn't holding back a shriek. "Wait a minute, wait just one minute, here! You want to stick me back a year? With . . . " I couldn't believe it! Not only was I yanked from my friends and home and school and everything just so Brother could do the scholar exchange thing, not only was I going to have to start a whole new school where I had no friends, but I had to be put back a year, too? Aaaaack! The idea was so horrible, I almost couldn't face it. "You want to stick me back with . . . with sophomores? But I'm a junior!"

"Emily, academically—"

"I won't do it!"

"The school system here is different than back home—"

"I WON'T DO IT!" Honestly, Dru, I hated to make a scene in front of Hottie A. I mean, what would he think of me? But being put back a year on top of everything else . . . well, I just kind of lost it at that point.

"It's all been settled, sweetling."

"Do you have *any* concept of just how much you have ruined my life?" I yelled, really freaking.

Mom came in at that point, which is probably a good thing, because you know, I really didn't want Aidan to see me murder my father—or worse, burst into tears. Either way he'd probably get the wrong idea about me. Anyway, Mom came in and asked with that *ignore Emily making a scene* face how things were going.

"That man you married has just killed any future I have whatsoever! He wants me to go to school with *sophomores!*"

Aidan, hunk of my dreams, smiled again. Could he be any more adorable? I think not. "It's not that bad, Emily." I stopped in mid freak-out. He said my name! My name was on his lips! "Fifth form is all right. You get to swot for whatever subjects you like for the GSCE."

"But we won't be in the same classes, then, will we?"

"Well, no," he said, doing the finger-on-the-mustache thing again. "I'll be taking different sorts of classes than you. Sixth formers study for their A levels, while the fifth form studies for the GSCE. That stands for General Certificate of Secondary Education. A levels are what you take to go to university."

"It sounds like a stupid system," I muttered, loud enough for Brother to hear. If he thought I was going to let him shove me back with mere children, he could just think again. I decided, however, that it wouldn't be at all a smooth move to make my point in front of Aidan. He probably already thought I was a little weird. So I gritted my loins and girded my teeth and all that.

Then Mom said . . .

Sorry, had to answer the Parental Call. Like they can't walk in here to talk to me? I have to leave, we're going out shopping for my school uniform before the stores close. I tried what you suggested, but Amnesty International said they don't think being forced to wear a school uniform qualifies as a cruel and unusual punishment.

More later. I'm not through telling you about Aidan yet, and there's tomorrow . . . must go. Evidently my mother is going to have a heart attack and die if we don't leave right now. Let me know if you've left the house yet, and how the Zombie family maid burned down their house.

Hs and Ks,
~Em

Subject: I am never going to live through this year
From: Mrs.Oded@btelecom.co.uk
To: Dru@seattlegrrl.com
Date: 3 September 2003 8:50 pm

> Maybe it won't be as bad as you think, maybe . . .
> oh, what am I saying? Of course it will be bad! I can't
> imagine going back to tenth grade! That would be
> awful. I think you have grounds to sue your parents
> for mistreatment.

I'm back. I survived, although just barely, the trip to Valentine's, a scabby old store in glorious downtown Piddlesville that caters to the Indentured School Slaves. The woman who runs the teen area had big poofy pink hair that looked just like cotton candy, and she kept calling me "dearie." It was awful.

Before I describe the horrors that are now hanging in my wardrobe, let me tell you about POTW. First off, it's very small, which is no surprise, because I can't imagine anyone who wants to live in a city with that name. There's a High Street with a couple of cool shops, and a handful of grotty shops ("grotty" is a local word. It means grotesque. IMHO, there's a lot about POTW that's on the grotty side), a Second Street with gas stations and a McDonald's, and that's about it. Valentine's is the local department store, although how anyone can even think of buying anything there is one of those mysteries that will never get solved. The clothes in the window were so eighties I almost heard the theme to *Knots Landing*. Inside was even worse—it was dim and dusty and the wooden floor creaked, and the whole place smelled like old cabbage and mothballs.

"If this is what my life has come to," I said, stopping and refusing to go any farther once I saw the school uniforms, "then you can kill me now. Please. It'll be a merciful ending, no one will blame you."

"Tempting as that offer is, I think we'll just settle for getting you kitted out," Mom said, pulling out a list the school had sent her.

Kitted out? Even my mother has gone English. Clearly it's up to me to take a stand and be the last bastion of Americanism in my family. Well, except for using cool words like grotty. Grotty is good.

Mom dragged me over to a rack of horrible maroon clothes and consulted the List. I swear, Dru, only the fact that everyone else at this horrible Butt-mouth school I'm being forced to attend will be wearing the same thing is keeping me from taking Mom's Visa card and going home.

Since I have nothing else to do, I'll attach the list here so you can suffer with me.

Gobottom Senior Girls School Uniform

Item: Blazer
Description: Maroon, with school emblem
What I think: The school emblem looks like one of those spaceship/satellite thingies from the seventies that were all pointy legs and bits of aluminum poking out at odd angles. I have no idea what it's supposed to be. And maroon? Give me a friggin' break! Maroon sucks! Who looks good in maroon? Who can color-coordinate around maroon? Maroon makes me look like I'm going to barf.

Item: School tie
Description: Maroon and teal diagonal stripes.
What I think: It's crap!
"A tie?" I asked Mom when she held one up. "Excuse me, but I am not a male. I don't wear ties."
She shoved it in the basket, muttering something about the colors hurting her eyes. Fine. I might have to wear it, but no one said where. I think I'll wear it around my waist, under my clothes. A tie! Can you even *imagine* it? And who came up with the combination of maroon and teal, two utterly gross colors that together are so repulsive they can strike people dead a half mile away?

Item: Blouse
Description: White. (Note, blouse is a normal-style shirt, not baggy with a soft collar.)
What I think: Honestly, Dru, it's terrible. The material

is thirty percent polyester, and you know I can't wear polyester. It doesn't breathe! You wouldn't think a white blouse would be a problem, would you? I have tons of white tops. I pointed that out to Mom, but according to the Pink Hair, "The school is ever so particular what the girls wear. If you don't want a demerit, dearie, you just stay with the standard blouse."

Great. I'm going to look like a geek. A tie and a stupid white blouse.

Question: Can my life get any worse?
Answer: Don't make me laugh.

Item: Skirt
Description: Teal, pleated all around, knee-length
What I think: It looks like something my grandmother wears to church. Knee-length? I don't think so. Thank heavens I took Home Ec last year and learned how to hem. The hemline on this puppy is going up several inches.

Item: Tights
Description: Heavy black tights or white/gray knee socks.
What I think: White socks with a skirt? WHITE SOCKS WITH A SKIRT? Are they out of their minds? And heavy black tights (tights are nylons)? Black, yes, black is chic, black is slimming, black is cool, but the tights the Pink Lady brought out were positively hairy, they were so thick! I let Mom buy them, but just as soon as I find a real store, I'm buying some proper black nylons.

Item: Shoes

Description: Black with low heels

What I think: Ha ha ha ha ha! Low heels, my Aunt Fanny!

There's optional teal "trousers" (do these people have a different word for everything?) that I could get, but they are worse than the skirt, and besides, with a skirt I can show off my legs. So I nixed the trousers. Then there's the PE stuff—a white polo shirt with the stupid school logo that's not too hideous, maroon bicycle shorts that are going to let everyone see that I need to lose ten more pounds, a teal "games skirt" that I refuse to even think about (it's for tennis and hockey. Right, like I want to play hockey in a miniskirt. What sort of pervs made up this list?), boots for hockey and "football" (another example of the English getting it backward—football here means soccer), and white tennis shoes, called, for some inexplicable reason, "trainers."

Oh, poop, BRB.

Back! I had to answer the phone, since the Oldsters were too busy examining something in the basement (blocking up the portal to hell that's no doubt down there). Bess is in Liverpool. She says she's met a "bloke" (you see? I'm the only one who hasn't been Englishized) who's evidently really hot, and he's taking her to see some Beatles museum or something.

OHMIGOD! I just went upstairs to get the digital camera so I could take some pictures for you of this mausoleum The Parents are forcing me to live in, and my underwear was all over the floor again! It was too creepy! I just stood there in the room and felt invaded! I've got to think of some way to beat this pervy ghost, Dru. You can help me. You're a Pisces, you're good at all that mystical stuff. Work me up a spell or something, would you?

OK, so back to yesterday and Aidan. After Mom came into the room, they started talking about school stuff until Mom turned to Aidan and literally saved my life.

"Emily is dying to visit the nearest mall, Aidan. Can you tell me where it is? She won't be happy until she checks out all of the stores."

"Mall?" he asked, his adorable eyebrows pulling together in an adorable frown that was just so . . . well, *adorable*.

"Yeah, you know, a bunch of stores and restaurants and sometimes movie theaters and stuff where you hang out?"

"Hang out?" He blinked at me. "There's Valentine's and other shops in town here, or Alling."

A horrible cold, clammy feeling twisted my stomach into a ball. I grabbed Aidan's sleeve, not even getting the slightest thrill at touching his arm. "Are you trying to say . . . you can't mean . . . you're not telling me . . . there's *no mall?*"

OK, I admit my voice was a bit squeaky by the time it got to the last words, but still, that was no reason for him to look at me like I had a great big zit right in the middle of my forehead.

"There's shops in town," he repeated, taking a step back.

It was an effort, but I managed to get a grip on myself enough to A) not barf on him, and B) not scream. But I wanted to do both. Yeah, yeah, I know, malls aren't as important as something like world peace, but tell me this: where do the kids here go if they don't have a mall to hang out at? You know me, I'm not a shopaholic, but malls are *necessary*. Where else can you hang with all your friends and eat and flirt with the guys? I mean, what sort of weird country HAS NO MALLS? I swear I started hyperventilating. I definitely saw spots before my eyes, but before I could actually pass out, I did a bit of deep breathing, and I'm glad I did. It paid off, big time.

"If you like, I can show you round the shops," Aidan said. I stopped panicking and immediately adopted an interested—but not too desperate—look.

"Oh," I said, toying with a moldy book sitting on an end table. The world as I knew it settled back into its normal . . . um . . . ness. Maybe kids here hang out at the shops? Regardless, Aidan offering to show me around them was a Good Thing. "Thanks. That would be cool."

"Thursday?" he asked, his mustache smiling at me.

"Sure," I answered, trying hard not to grab him and kiss him in front of The Ancients.

He nodded and Mom said thank-you and gushed over him for a little bit. (It was disgusting. I think she's having a midlife crisis or something. I'm going to have to have a talk with her, too.) Then the dean gave me another denture grin, and Aidan smiled and said he'd pick me up at two, and they left.

I hope you're absolutely dying with jealousy! I have a date tomorrow with a mustached hottie who wants to show me "round the shops." So, the big question is, what should I wear? You know what I brought with me, tell me what you think. What should I say? Should I be bold or shy? I'm off to a bad start, what with him thinking I'm so juvenile I have to be put back with the fifth formers, so I really want to emphasize my maturity. Should I wear my Wonderbra, or do you think that's too much too soon? And what if he tries to kiss me? Should I let him, or should I act casual and not really interested? What if he wants to do more? What if he wants to do *it*? OHMIGOD, can you imagine *it* with him? I think I'm going to melt, I really do. I'd better go take a bath. I'm steaming up the computer monitor.

Before I go, I wanted to remind you to tell me what's going on with you. I know I've been kind of focused on my life in hell, but I want to know what's happening to you, as well. I can't believe you haven't left the house for five whole days! You must be going mad! Tell all. Oh, and the thing with the fire department in The Sims—I told you before, you have to have a smoke detector near the stove, or else the fire department won't come. That's why the Zombies' house burned down. Too bad about Renaldo Zombie, but you know, Morticia can do better. Send her on vacation to see what hottie Sims are hanging around the pool in Speedos.

Later!

Hugs and kisses,
~Em

Subject: Re: What about Oded, hmmm?
From: Mrs.Oded@btelecom.co.uk
To: Dru@seattlegrrl.com
Date: 4 September 2003 6:13 pm

> *think you're right after all. If he saw you in sweats*
> *yesterday, you'll want to show him that you don't*
> *look like a slob all of the time. I think the batik skirt*
> *and halter will say just what you want it to say.*

I looked fabulous!

> *Tell me everything, EVERYTHING about the date!*

It was fabulous!

> *Tell me what he said!*

He was fabulous!

> *And be sure to tell me if he tries to kiss you!*

Well, he wasn't *that* fabulous.

> *There's nothing going on here, I can't go anywhere*
> *until the cast is off. Just keep telling me what's*
> *happening to you. And tell me more about Aidan!*

I can't believe nothing is happening—even with a broken leg you can cause endless trouble—but since you're
probably going stir-crazy and need distracting so you
don't stick a coat hanger down your cast, I'll spill. Yes,
everything, despite the slob comment. You're just
insanely jealous of my fabulous date with Aidan.

He picked me up in his dad's car (which explained the
scent of Old that permeated everything) and drove to
greater downtown POTW, which, as I mentioned, basically consists of two streets. He parked near a bank, and
we trotted down the street, stopping at a couple of the
cool shops. As I said before, there aren't very many!

Once we had done that and looked at the sights (an
old church, a graveyard, and a post thingy that some
king put up a long time ago), Aidan asked me if I'd like

to stop by the local for a butty.

"Local what?" I asked, wondering if a butty was like a botty. Yes, Dru, only in England will you find that even the smallest town has a local butt shop.

"Pub," he said.

"Cool!" I said. Unfortunately, this weird country allows you in a pub if you're not eighteen, but they won't let you drink. You have to buy food. Even so, Aidan managed to get us shandies, which is kind of like a real drink—it's half beer and half fizzy lemonade. I'm not sure if we were allowed to drink them or not, but I didn't want to look like a boob and ask Aidan. To be honest, it wasn't very good, but you know me, I am ever coolio, so I drank it. Aidan also bought us each a sandwich, which for some reason is called a butty here—I will never understand these people. He told me about what he's going to be studying this year, and just when he asked me what I did back home, a couple of his friends rolled up.

"Those are my mates," he said, waving his sandwich/butty at two guys. I gave them the eye (you know the old saying: one hunk is good, but three are better). One of them was very tall, with dark brown hair and brown puppy-dog eyes, and the other was blue-eyed and had really short black hair with very cool blond tips on the ends.

"That's Fang," Aidan said, pointing at the tall puppy-dog guy, "and Devon. This is Emily. She's going to Gobbotty this year. Her dad's a visiting scholar."

"Poor lass," Devon said, twirling a chair around and sitting down with the back to his front. It was such a smooth move! I gave him my very best smile, and prayed there was no bit of butty on my teeth. "I wouldn't wish

Gob-botty on anyone. In the sixth form then, are you?"

Why did *everyone* have to ask me that?

"I should be," I answered, putting my martyred look on. "But my dad's an idiot and he signed me up for the fifth form."

Devon grimaced and stole a potato chip from my plate (oh, wait, they're called crisps here. Like they couldn't just say potato chip?), giving me a completely heart-stopping grin as he did. "Don't mind, do you? I'm a bit fagged. Here, Fang, get us a pint."

OHMIGOD! He just called himself a . . . no, I must have heard him wrong. Fang, who had just sat down, got up again and went to the bar.

"What's up, Aid?" Devon asked, stealing another chip. I pushed my plate toward him and told him to knock himself out.

"Not much, just been showing Emily the shops. Devon's starting college this year," Aidan told me. That explained why Devon could order a pint—he must be eighteen.

"That's right," he said, taking a huge glass of beer from Fang. "Engineering. Good money to be made there."

"If you're with the right company, sure. But you can make more through R and D with some of the big conglomerates than you can in practical engineering."

"Ho-ho, will you look at the girl talk." Devon laughed, setting down his pint. He leaned forward and grabbed my hand. "Now what would a fair thing like yourself know about research and development?"

Why is it that boys think they are the only ones who can understand science? "I happen to have been scheduled to take a year of advanced study in math and physics, but now that's off because I'm here. I'm going to be a physicist. Practical, not theoretical," I added.

"Brainy bird," Devon said, pulling my hand up to his mouth. I thought for one horrible moment he was going to bite me, but all he did was kiss my knuckles. Which was very cool in itself, but it would have been much cooler if I hadn't been so miffed at him. Still, he did kiss my hand, and he was cute, and eighteen, and all. So I decided to forgive him.

The guys talked about their jobs for a bit (Devon was the only one who didn't work, but I gathered from the hints that Aidan dropped that his parents had a lot of money, and he didn't need to work), and about friends I didn't know. Fang was pretty quiet, only speaking when the other guys asked him a question, but he smiled and laughed with them. It turns out he is older than both of them, nineteen, and is already going to college. He's studying to be a vet, which is really nice, don't you think?

Everything was lovely—me at a table with three hunkables hanging on my every word—until *she* came in.

"There you are, love," this tall blond said as she glared at me for a moment, then leaned over and planted her lips on Aidan. Right in front of me! Deliberately! On *my* date! "I've been looking for you. I thought you were taking me to the flicks tonight?"

Aidan shot me a quick look but didn't say anything when she plopped herself down in his lap. "Erm . . . that's not until later, Tash."

"No harm in getting started early, is there? Who's your little friend?"

Now, let me describe this witch so you can understand just how obnoxious she is—first of all, she wasn't so much taller than me that she had any right to call me little. Maybe a few inches taller, but that's it. Yes, she had on a really cool leather skirt, thigh-high boots, and a studded leather choker, but her lipstick was TOTALLY wrong for her coloring (hair was dyed, natch). She sat snuggling up to *my* potential boyfriend, cooing at him and touching him and blowing in his ear.

Aidan looked really uncomfortable. Obviously he was too much of a gentleman to push her off his lap, which says a lot about him. Unless he liked her there . . . you don't think that was it, do you? Naw, it couldn't be. She was clearly not at all his type. He was just being polite.

"Emily, this is Tash. She's Devon's cousin." And the judges take fifty points away from Devon. "Emily's from the States."

"And she's going to be a physicist," Fang said. I gave him my second-best smile, the one where I don't let my eyes twinkle. He grinned back. He might not be as hunkable as Aidan and Devon, but he has really nice eyes and he likes animals. So I'll keep him on my Possible BF list.

"Isn't she sweet, though," Tash drawled.

OH! Sweet? Me? Ha! I'll show her sweet!

"Tash works at the beauty salon next to Garfinkles," Aidan said.

Garfinkles was the closest thing to a trendy shop in Piddle-me-silly-ton. It had a lot of Goth gear, which no doubt explained Tash's obvious leather fetish.

"Yes, do come round sometime," she positively purred, turning her shoulder so her left boob rubbed up against poor Aidan. I just know he hated it. "I'm sure we can do *something* with your hair."

OHMIGOD! Now, you *know* my hair is one of my weak

points, but for her to say that in front of everyone . . . !
I'm going to get her for that, Dru, oh yes, I am.

However, having been raised in a civilized country, and
not being at all a snotty, slime-toed she-devil, I smiled as
nicely as I could, but the rest of the afternoon was
ruined. Tash stuck to Aidan like a tick on a hairy dog,
and even Devon winking at me twice, and calling me a
bird (the guys here evidently have a thing about calling
girls birds, which is really kind of cute, don't you think?)
didn't make up for her ruining the day.

The one good thing that happened was that Devon
told Aidan he would take me home, but Aidan insisted
that he do it. It was utterly fabu having two droolworthy guys fighting over who would take me home, but
unfortunately Tash refused to leave Aidan, so we had to
suffer her riding along with us. She beat me to the front
seat, too, which just goes to show you how insecure
she is. Still, she works during the day, and he'll be at
Gobstoppers with me, so my life doesn't look totally
hopeless.

I prolly won't be able to e-mail you for a couple of
days. Brother is dragging us to the Lake District (supposed to be scenic—although scenery doesn't thrill
me, as long as there are no libraries around, I'll be
happy) for a long weekend. And then the hellish
nightmare of fifth form starts on Monday, but I'll talk
to you before then.

Have you tried driving yet with the cast? Who else has
signed it? What about Vance? Is he back from Chicago?
Has he tried to get jiggy with you yet? Inquiring minds
need to know! What's happening with your Sims? Tell
me, tell me, tell me! I miss you guys!

Hugs and kisses,
~Em

Subject: I was *SO* right!
From: Mrs.Oded@btelecom.co.uk
To: Dru@seattlegrrl.com
Date: 7 September 2003 4:22 pm

I always am, aren't I? Well, OK, there was the year I
thought having my nipple pierced would be really cool,
but I soon saw the error in THAT thinking.

The famed Lake District was just a bunch of green
hills, water, and trees and stuff. Nothing to write home
about, although I guess technically I'm doing just that.
Still, I survived four days stuffed in a car with the 'rents
while they drove around and oohed and aahed over the
scenery. It was OK, but there weren't any castles or
other cool stuff to see. Joy of joys, the stuff we shipped
out before we left Seattle was here when we returned
to Mansion du Ghastly. Mom is happy because now she
has her own towels (I'll never understand her), Brother
has his books, Bess—back from jaunting around
England on her own, the brat—has her laptop, and I
have the rest of my makeup, hot rollers, the big hair
dryer, and of course, my Sims. Where would I be without my Sims? Brother kicked up a bit of a fuss when he
saw how much room it took up on the hard drive, but I
soon set him straight.

"*Who* told me we could bring only one computer with
us?" I asked righteously.

"I wasn't about to pay the shipping and import duty
on two computers—" Brother started to say, but I cut
him off.

"And yet *who* let one of the fruits of his loins bring her laptop?"

"Your sister paid for her own laptop to be sent—"

"And *who* promised me that it would be just fine for all of us, minus the Favored Child, to use the same computer?"

"I simply asked you if you would leave me a little space on the computer so I can save my work. Your silly games aren't necessary to our health and happiness, but my notes and assignments are."

I straightened up to my full height and glared up at him. Mom had made him brush out his hair horn, but he still looked goofy. "The Sims is not silly and it's not a game, Unibrow. It's a simulation of people and their families and friends and dates and neighbors. You can build a house, decorate it, and then make Sim people to live in it. It's realistic! It's all about interaction and relationships and family units and all that stuff that you Oldsters are always going on about, and everyone who is even remotely cool and has good taste loves it. If you are finished ruining the last shreds of happiness in my pitiful life, you may leave."

Despite my shooing him away, he stood there with a really confused look on his face. "Unibrow?"

I sniffed and loaded up the SimWilliams family. It was time to let the Grim Reaper have his way with SimBrother.

"Did you just call me Unibrow?"

"If the unibrow fits, wear it," I told the computer.

He shook his head and left the library, muttering things about blood tests and paternity lawsuits. I ignored him, of course.

As I told you, Bess has arrived. She made a big deal

about it, too, zooming up to the House of Horrors on the back of a motorbike. The guy she was with looked like he was a hippie or Jesus or something—long brown beard, long scraggly hair, no fashion sense, etc. Bess introduced him to Brother as some sort of a monk, but you know Bess—she's as radical as they come. Anyhoodles, after Monk left, and Bess had her hissy fit about me getting the tower room—which I told her came with an underwear-obsessed ghost—she came stomping into the bathroom later and demanded to talk to me.

"Excuse me, do you notice that I'm A) naked, and B) taking a bath?" I asked. She just sat on the toilet and started poking through my trays of makeup.

"I remember you in diapers, squirt, so don't get uppity with me." She picked up one of my concealers and squinted at it. "Don't you know this stuff is nothing but a waste of money?"

I gasped. Concealer? A waste of money? Well, yeah, maybe for her with her perfect skin and her perfect face it was a waste of money, but the rest of us had to make the best of what we had.

"I hope this is not tested on animals," she added as she shook the container, then set it down to open up the case containing my 110 different shades of eye shadow. "I don't know why you have to wear so much makeup, Em. It's not like you're ugly. I guess it's just a phase you're going through. When you get older like me, you'll realize that you don't really need it."

I ground my teeth as I fluffed up my diminishing bath bubbles. I *hated* it when she got all worldly older sister on me. She was only two years older!

"This stuff will clog your pores if you wear it all the

time. You're much better off allowing your skin to breathe. If you keep slapping on the makeup the way you do, you'll look like you're fifty before you're twenty-five."

I turned on the hot water with my toes. "Thank you so much for the advice, but my skin breathes just fine. Did you want something in particular, or are you just trying to see me naked?"

She rolled her eyes and set down my blush. "I've seen you naked, stupid. It's nothing to get excited about. I wanted to know if you'd like to come with me next weekend. I'm going to Suffolk with a bunch of others to protest the nuclear plant there."

"No, thank you." My sister, the radical political activist. She caught me once in that trap, I wasn't about to let her do it again. Good causes are all well and fine, but the people she hangs out with are always so . . . *intense*. Besides, I had enough to cope with right now. I soaped up my fwoofy soap thing and prepared to shave my right leg.

"The government wants to build a new generation of nuclear power plant, rather than using renewable resources like solar and wind power."

"Uh-huh." I resoaped, then shaved my left leg. "Poop, the razor's going dull. Would you hand me a new one?"

She tapped her finger on my hot rollers. "A recent poll showed that more than seventy percent of the people responding said they preferred renewable energies rather than new nuclear power stations."

"Yes, well, that's all very interesting, but right now I'm in full crisis mode, and if I have to go to my new school with hairy legs, I'm going to fall right over and die. Razor, please?"

She handed me a new razor. I recommended shaveage.

"In addition, a recent study found that forty wind farms off the eastern coast of England could produce as much energy as all of the nuclear power plants in Britain put together, plus the creation of such wind farms would generate sixty thousand new jobs."

I sighed. Once Bess gets going about something, she never lets up. "You're forgetting one important thing." I raised my arm for pit shaving.

She frowned. "What's that?"

"You're not British. Why should you be telling them what to do with their country?"

She *tch*ed and rolled her eyes and made that annoyed face that she always seems to make around me and no one else. "Emily, the day will come when you're going to have to learn that—"

I stopped shaving my armpit and finished the sentence with her. "—that we're all living in a global village, and that means we have to care for each other, no matter what our nationality."

She stuck her tongue out at me, which was a *really* juvenile thing to do. I threw my fwoofy soapy thing at her. As if it's not bad enough I have a father who thinks everything medieval is cool, I get stuck with a perfect sister who spends a couple of days in England and she's already made a ton of friends, and has a BF, and doesn't need to wear makeup to look good, and doesn't get put back a grade, and most of all, she can do whatever she wants just because she's two years older than me! Mom and I are the only normal ones in the family, and sometimes I have my doubts about her.

Speaking of that, I used my time trapped in the car

with Them to open up negotiations about school. Unfortunately, Brother claims there's nothing he can do, that he sent the headmaster (Sounds kind of bondage-y and kinky, doesn't it? I bet this headmaster guy is the perv who thought up girls wearing miniskirts during hockey) my grades for last year, and the HM said I had to go into the fifth form because I hadn't taken my SATs yet. Well of course I haven't! That's supposed to happen next spring! Evidently only kids who are planning to go to college are allowed into the sixth form. If I had taken the SATs—which would mean I was serious about going to college—then the headmaster of this school might have bent the rules, but instead I'm being punished because we don't take the SATs until spring. How unfair is that? Mega unfair! So despite the fact that I have a 3.8 GPA, despite the fact that I was scheduled to have a whole year of AP classes, despite all that, I get shoved back into the equivalent of tenth grade.

It's going to be hell. Pity me, Dru. Come tomorrow, I'll be a sophomore again.

An American sophomore.

One who's a whole year older than everyone else.

And I won't know a single, solitary person!

Sniffle.

Catch me up on everything that's happened while I've been gone. As for Vance—forget him. You can do better! He's a creep if he can't see that you are the perfect girl for him. I'm sorry he made you cry—if you like, I can ask Tommy Delarosa to break his kneecaps. Bet that would teach him a thing or two. E-mail me as soon as you get up.

Hugs and kisses,
~Em

Subject: OMG!!!!!!!!!!!!!!!!!!!!!!!!!!!
From: Mrs.Oded@btelecom.co.uk
To: Dru@seattlegrrl.com
Date: 8 September 2003 3:36 pm

Before I get to your trouble with V, you have to hear about my day. I have never, ever, *ever* been so humiliated in my whole, entire, horrible life! Dru, I could die, I could just die! I almost got expelled! On my first day! All because of some STUPID rules some STUPID person made for this STUPID school. I cried in the bathroom, and you know I *never* cry in the bathroom! That's always been a code of mine, hasn't it?

Let me tell you what happened—I got dressed in the horrible maroon and teal uniform and then, of course, I had to think seriously about what makeup to apply that wouldn't clash with it. Visualize the girl: I wore Kiss Me Mauve lipstick, Moonlit Teal eyeliner, Nautical Navy shadow (highlighted with Crisp Linen shadow), Raven mascara (I know you think I'm too blond for Raven, but I'm thinking of coloring my hair darker), and Glamora blush, with just a really light dusting of bronzing powder. Tasteful and yet subdued, yes?

Unfortunately, not even having all my makeup on made me feel good. But despite being so nervous I could barf, I trotted downstairs. Mom was waiting for me. "My, don't you look . . . eh . . . yes. All set to go?"

I didn't make a face because I didn't want the Kiss Me Mauve to go all over my teeth, so I confined myself to a Look. "You can't be serious! You don't expect me to have my *mother* take me to school the first day. I have my reputation to think about! Do you want me to be a hermit for the rest of my life?"

"No, of course not, but I hardly see how my driving

you to school is going to ostracize you from your friends."

"I don't have any friends here, that's just the point," I said, grabbing my purse and PDA. Mom made a hurt face, so I decided to give in. "Oh, all right, if you absolutely insist, you can drive me, but you have to let me out a couple of blocks away so no one sees me with you."

"Thank you, Emily. You've made me feel so special."

Mom dropped me off a block from the school. We had to wait for a bit until there was no one who could see me get out of the car, but I made it there without anyone spotting her. I toddled in to the office to check in per instructions from Brother.

"Are you Williams?" a tall, dark-haired girl came up and asked me. She wore a little hat, had the end of her tie tucked into her shirt, and carried a clipboard.

I smiled my nicest smile (the one where I look like Christina Aguilera) at her. "Yep."

"Thought so." She eyed me from my toes to my hair, and wrinkled up her nose like she smelled something bad. "You look like an American."

"Really?" I glanced down at myself. I wasn't wearing anything with stars and stripes.

"Yes, really. Could you *have* on more makeup?"

I blinked at her, totally blown away. I mean, all I said was hi, and she started jumping all over me! It was like some horrible first-day-of-school nightmare that I couldn't wake up from.

You'd be proud of me, Dru. I didn't say one mean thing to her, I just raised my chin and looked down my nose at her like she wasn't worth the trouble to talk to. Well, OK, if I'm being truthful—and you know I always am with you—I didn't say anything because I couldn't think of what to say. Which should tell you just how shocked I was.

"What's the matter, cat got your tongue? Oh, it's no matter, it's better if you don't talk. Follow me. I'm the prefect for the fifth form. You have to go to your form room before lessons start."

"What*ever*," I said, trying hard to look like I didn't want to cry.

BTW, I have no idea what prefect means, unless it's "evil, bossy girl who sucked up to some teacher until she was made Official Teacher's Pet."

"Right, pay attention Williams. I'm only going to do this once. Those are the ICT rooms," Duff the OTP said, pointing down a hallway. "Over there is maths, history, general studies, and Latin."

Uck. A school with Latin. Like living with Brother spouting Latin every opportunity he gets isn't enough torture?

We went up a flight of stairs to the second floor. Most of the other kids looked OK—definitely younger than me—but all of them turned around to stare when we passed. Either they'd never seen anyone wear the ghastly school uniform with such coolness or else the Duff was right, and I look somehow different. Do you think . . . no, never mind. If there's one thing I know, it's makeup, right? Right.

"Down there is Religious Ed and Sociology. This is Mod Lang, and to the right is the science wing."

"Mod Lang?"

She sighed like it was such a hard thing to talk to me. "Mod Lang as in Modern Languages. This will be your form room. You're to report here every morning for registration and assembly."

She stopped in front of the door and turned to squint her mean little eyes at me. "Gobottle School doesn't allow students to wear cosmetics, so you'd best wipe that off before the head of form sees you. She doesn't tolerate sluts in her class. Girls' lavatory is at the end of the hall."

Slut! I am *so* not a slut! I really wanted to tell her off, but figured that she had to be the school bully, and you know how school bullies are—if I ignored her, I'd show her that she was a tiny little speck of dog poop that didn't matter in the least to me.

There were about twenty others standing around in the room, mostly girls (just my luck, although I don't know why I care, they're all younger than me, and you know I don't go for younger men), so I sat down to wait and see what the routine was. In walked this tall, horsey woman—I mean, she had a long face like a horse, and her hair kind of looked like a mane—and the first thing she did was point a long, horsey finger at me and said, "You! What's your name?"

"Emily Williams," say I, über-coolio despite a woobidy stomach and being called a slut.

She sniffed, kind of like she smelled cooked cabbage or something, and gave me the eye. "You're the Yank. Well, Williams, there are a few rules you will learn immediately. First, we do *not* sit until the teacher has given you permission to sit. We do *not* wear our school tie tied into a bow. We do *not* wear necklaces, rings, or other jewelry. We do *not* wear cosmetics."

Everyone in the class laughed at me. Honestly, Dru, it was so humiliating I didn't know whether I wanted to cry or scream. In the end I decided that I would die before I let them see that I cared what they thought. So I pretended to yawn.

"Lester, you will please show Williams the girls' loo so she can wash off her face. You will remove all jewelry except your watch." She peered closely at me, her beady little eyes getting even beadier. "And that includes all of those earrings that are studding your ear. Do your parents know you have them?"

I stood up when a rabbity girl tugged on my sleeve. Everyone looked at me like I was some sort of a freak! Me! I did the only thing I could do. I said, "Well, duh!"

She pulled herself up and snorted (just like a horse). "We do *not* address our superiors in any tone but that of respect."

I decided the time had come to make a stand. You know me, I'm the most reasonable person on the face of the earth, but when some old poop starts to push me around and tell me to take my earrings out, that's it!

"We?" I said, striking a very cool pose of utter indifference even though I was seething inside. "What, you have a pocketful of worms? For your information, I don't take my earrings out for anyone. If I did, the holes would close, and it took me eight months to get all five holes pierced. And as for respect, I give it to people who've earned it."

So, OK, in hindsight that might not have been the best thing to say, but Brother always said I should never let anyone trample my rights and to stand up for what was important to me, so really, I was just doing what he taught me.

Everyone in the classroom gasped. Miss Horseface gave a snort that rattled the windows, then she grabbed me in one horsey claw and dragged me out of the room and down the stairs to the office. Right in front of everyone! I wanted to die. *Again*.

I had to sit there for fifteen minutes while she talked to headmaster. Then Horseface opened the door and waved me in. The HM guy looked a bit like Russell Crowe, although much older and not nearly so cute. Still, he was cute enough that even though I was utterly miserable, I was glad I'd put on Kiss Me Mauve rather than Notice Me Mauve.

"Miss Williams, I'm Mr. Krigon. I understand from Miss Naylor that there's a bit of confusion about what Gobottle School expects from you. Won't you sit down?" He smiled a really nice smile that made me feel a little better, and held the door open as he shooed Horse Woman out. "Thank you, Miss Naylor. I'll let you return to the students. I'll show Miss Williams to her lesson one room."

Horsey snorted again, shot me a look that pretty much said she didn't expect anything but trouble from me, and stalked out of the room.

CRAP! Brother has to use the computer—it's some life or death emergency with an article or something. I'll finish up as soon as he's done.

More in a bit!

Hugs and kisses,
~Em

Subject: Take my father, please!
From: Mrs.Oded@btelecom.co.uk
To: Dru@seattlegrrl.com
Date: 8 September 2003 4:17 pm

Brother's crisis du jour is over, so I'm back. I wish you were home now so you could scream with me about the horrible time I had at school.

Let's see, I left off with me and Mr. Russell Crowe Krigon in his office, right? Well, he was actually very sweet, although I can't help but wonder about the miniskirts-in-hockey thing. And I haven't forgiven him yet for not letting me in the sixth form. He told me that the school has a dress code that goes beyond the uniform, and that I was allowed to wear only *one* pair of earrings. One! Have you ever heard of anything so barbaric?

"You may wear what you have on for the rest of the day, but in the future, please remember to remove them before you leave home."

I thought about telling him my holes would close up if I went running around without earrings, but it was just too embarrassing to be talking about my earlobes to him, so I let it go.

He also asked me to remove most of my makeup (notice he didn't say *all*), and he even winked at me when he said that. He didn't say one single thing about me looking like a whore, so I knew that was just the Duff being nasty. Since Mr. Krigon asked so nicely, I humored him, blotting the Kiss Me Mauve really hard, dabbing at the bronzed bits with a wet piece of paper towel, and even going so far as to take off the eye shadow (although I left the mascara and eyeliner, because you know my eyes just disappear into my face without mascara and eyeliner). He waited for me outside of the bathroom and didn't say anything when I came out, so I think the makeup issue is settled.

He asked me all sorts of questions about Seattle while

we walked up two flights of stairs, and told me he was impressed with my grades. "You'll be happy to know that our physical sciences department is quite comprehensive. I know that you got off to a bit of a bad start with Miss Naylor, but I'm sure you'll be very happy in her physics class."

Naylor? Horseface was the physics teacher? The woman who hated my guts and humiliated me in front of everyone? I groaned and mentally struck physics off the list of classes I was looking forward to. "Um. Yeah. I hope she doesn't hold grudges. I was hoping I could skip the first year and a half of college physics, so I really want to concentrate on learning what I can now."

"A commendable attitude to have," he said, and I couldn't help but feel hopeful. OK, so the day didn't start off very good, but it couldn't get any worse, right? Just as I was thinking that a bell went off and all sorts of kids started coming out of the rooms, and he said good-bye and left me outside the room.

Oh, you asked about my schedule. Here it is:

Lesson 1	English Lit

(Why they can't just say "class" is beyond me.)

Lesson 2	French
Lesson 3	PE
Lesson 4	Study
Lesson 5	Information Technology
Lunch	
Lesson 6	GSCE Maths
	(Why plural? Who knows!)
Lesson 7	GSCE Physics

(Evidently the GSCE classes are more intense, and intended for students who are specializing in that subject, kind of like an AP class. Which is cool, as long as our school gives me full credit for that.)

Lesson 8   Personal, Social, Citizenship,
                       and Health Education

You see the problem (other than the fact that Horse-face is going to fail me in physics), don't you? I knew you would. More about that later.

So anyway, there I was, marooned in maroon in my first class at a foreign school. Everyone was lined up outside of the class. No one went in. No one looked at me, no one said hi, no one said *anything* to me. It was like I wasn't there!

I turned to ask one of the girls in line what the deal was.

"Um, hi. Can you tell me what's going on? Why is everyone waiting outside the classroom?" I asked the nearest girl. She was tall and had braces, and big hoop earrings.

"*Um, hi,*" she mimicked me, like she was trying to sound American, only she totally didn't.

My stomach wadded up into a little ball as her friend giggled.

"Did you have fun at the headmaster's office?" the tall girl asked in one of those syrupy sweet voices that sound nice, but which everyone knows means she's being sarcastic.

Everyone in the line started snickering. I was beginning to wonder if there wasn't anyone normal at this school, but decided that whatever else happened, I wouldn't let on that their stupid comments mattered to me. They could stand on their heads and fart Yankee Doodle Dandy for all I cared! Nothing they did would matter to me. NOTHING!

Brother always says that the test of a person's mettle is how they handle adversity. If that's so, I'm the Queen Goddess of the World, because I didn't say one nasty thing. I just looked down my nose at the group of girls who snickered at me, and walked to the end of the line.

"Excuse me," I said with mega politeness to the one girl who wasn't laughing at me. It was the one named Lester who was in the form room when Miss Horse embarrassed me. "Is this the class for English Lit?"

"Yes, it is. I'm Holly Lester." She held out her hand, so I shook it, although I was halfway expecting her to start making fun of me, too. She didn't, though, and she seemed nice, although she had kind of a perpetually worried look on her face. "Did Mr. Krigon rip a strip off you?"

"Rip a strip? You mean yell at me? I'd like to see that!" She looked even more worried, so I toned my Brave Emily act down a bit. "Naw, he was actually very nice to me. He said he gets parents on his back if students don't all look the same, so he asked me to play along. Mondo boring, but you know how parents can be. I told him I would, although I'm going to be really PO'd if my holes close because of the stupid 'one set of earrings' rule."

"Oh." She looked at my ears, and her eyes got kind of glittery. "You have five earrings in each ear! That's . . . that's . . . "

"Coolio?" I asked, glaring at the two evil girls at the head of the line.

"Erm . . . I guess."

"Trust me, it is coolio. So if this is the English Lit class, why are we all standing outside rather than going in?"

Holly looked kind of scandalized, like I asked her to

dance naked down the hallway or something. "We always queue up before class."

"Oh, another one of those stup—" I stopped before I said the rest of the word. After all, just because it was her country, she wasn't responsible for the rules. She probably just didn't know that there was a much more reasonable way to do things. "Eh . . . silly rules. OK, so we stand around and wait for the teach to arrive. I'm copacetic with that. Maybe you can fill me in on what you guys do for fun. Those of you who aren't evil minions of Satan, that is," I added, shooting another glance at the girls who were poking each other and pointing at us. I was annoyed for a minute before I remembered that I didn't care what they did.

"Fun?" Holly asked, like she'd never heard of the word. Maybe she hadn't. She didn't look like she was overflowing with yucks. I tell you, Dru, I've never seen anyone who looked like such a scared rabbit. I just bet you that the evil girls had picked on her, too. I think I'm going to take her under my wing. Clearly she could use several million points on the cool scale, and since I know cool, I will just have to show her how to use it to handle the Snarky Sisters.

Where was I? Oh, yeah, so she says, "Fun?" like she didn't know what I was talking about.

"Yeah, you know, like what do you do during your study periods? That is, study lessons?" I figured I'd better not get into the whole period/lesson thing around her, in case she thought I meant Mister Monthly Visitor.

"We study."

"I mean, when you're not studying? Don't you guys have like a cool room where you hang out with all your friends, and put on makeup"— well, OK, scratch that

—"and gossip, and stuff?"

Her eyes got even bigger. "No, we don't."

A teacher, a little round butterball of a woman, rolled up. I smiled at Holly just before the teacher opened the door. "Well, we'll just have to change that, won't we?"

I thought her eyeballs were going to pop out of her head, but luckily La Femme Butterball herded everyone into the room (in a nice, orderly queue—*excuse me*, but I'm an adult, not a kindergartner!). I followed Holly to the back of the room, and stood like a nice little drone next to a desk until the B-ball told us we could sit.

Is it any wonder our four-score-and-seven-years-ago forefathers decided they'd had enough of this sort of totalitarian behavior? *Hello*, we're in the twenty-first century! Let's get with the times, people!

We all sat. I was just flipping open my PDA when all of a sudden the Butterball opens up her mouth and starts bellowing at the top of her lungs. "GOOD MORNING, CLASS. IT'S NICE TO SEE SO MANY FAMILIAR FACES BACK HERE THIS YEAR."

I stared at her for a moment, then glanced around the room. Other than the slightly dazed look on the faces of the kids in the first row, no one seemed to think anything of the fact that the teacher was yelling her brains out.

"BEFORE WE BEGIN THE CLASS, MARIAH WILL HAND OUT THE HOMEWORK TIMETABLE AND DIARY. YOU ARE RESPONSIBLE FOR UNDERTAKING YOUR COURSE-WORK ON A REGULAR AND SYSTEMATIC BASIS. DO NOT POSTPONE IT UNTIL YOU ARE NEAR THE DEAD-LINE. YOU WILL ALSO BE GIVEN YOUR GSCE PLAN-NING AND REVISION DIARY. THESE DIARIES ARE A VERY HELPFUL AID TO YOUR STUDY, SO DO NOT LOSE THEM."

There was a low-pitched humming noise in my ears. It was either a brain aneurysm, or I was going deaf.

"NOW WE WILL COMMENCE. THIS TERM WE WILL STUDY TWO OF SHAKESPEARE'S GREATEST WORKS—*ROMEO AND JULIET*, AND *HAMLET*. WE WILL BEGIN WITH *ROMEO AND* . . . YOU, GEL, YOU IN THE BACK WITH THE FRIZZY HAIR. WHAT IS THAT YOU HAVE?"

I looked around to see which of the frizzy-haired students she was bellowing at, then I realized it was me.

Frizzy hair? OHMIGOD, just shoot me, why don't you! Everyone in the class turned around to look at me (I really should be used to it by now), and remind me to e-mail the Pope, because I am most definitely next in line for sainthood. They all—with the exception of Holly, who looked worried—smiled smug little smiles at me. I couldn't help wondering why everyone was picking on my appearance. I looked just the same as I've always looked, and no one at home ever said anything nasty about my earrings or makeup. That's the one thing I know, right? I was feeling like enough was just about enough. I looked at the Butterball and cocked the Eyebrow of Questioning, and said, "Who, me?"

"YES, YOU, GEL. WHAT IS THAT IN YOUR HAND?"

I held up my hand. "Fingers?" Ten out of ten for style, huh?

"NO, NO, THE BLUE OBJECT."

I held up the PDA. "It's a PDA."

"A WHAT?"

I sighed and stood up. Evidently, in this country, if you stand, it makes people understand you. "PDA. That stands for Personal Digital Assistant. You do have them here, don't you?"

"THEY ARE NOT ALLOWED IN SCHOOL. PUT IT AWAY,

AND DO NOT BRING IT AGAIN."

The Bellowing Butterball turned toward the blackboard and started to write stuff, yelling at the top of her lungs all the while. The smarty-pants girls snickered at me a bit longer before turning back to the BB-ball. Holly was the only nice one in the class, and she looked like she wanted to cry for me.

"I'm so sorry," she said. "Don't mind Ann and Bertrice. They always act like that around anyone who's different."

Different? Now I was different? As in—*strange?*

I wanted to scream at all of them that *I* was not the uncool one, that I did not have frizzy hair, it was naturally curly, that I was not the one who spoke differently, they were, but I didn't. I just sat down, gritted my teeth, and took notes in my PDA (defiant to the end—that's something else Brother is big on).

I'll tell you about the rest of the classes after dinner. Once you get home, let me know what's going on back on the sane side of the world. I'm so bummed, I don't even want to Sims.

Hugs and kisses,
~Em

Subject: Re: You poor thing! You poor, poor thing!
From: Mrs.Oded@btelecom.co.uk
To: Dru@seattlegrrl.com
Date: 8 September 2003 11:11 pm

Dru wrote:
> *Connie carried my backpack for me, but you know*

> her, she's so Miss Transparent. I could tell she was
> just trying to schmooze up to me because she likes
> Vance. But I figured she couldn't do me any harm as
> my personal body slave. Vance called last night and
> apologized for standing me up. He said his car
> broke down.

Under no circumstances are you to forgive him! You're
much too good for him, Dru. He doesn't deserve your
love, not when he's out driving Tabitha around when he
promised to take you to the mall.

> I don't know how you survived! I would have
> melted into a puddle of tears. You are the bravest
> person I know, Em, you really are. I can't wait to
> hear what the rest of the classes were like.

They weren't too horrible, if you don't mind sitting in
classes with a bunch of children who hate your guts.
Holly (you remember her, she was the nice one) is in five
of my classes, which is good. Miss Naylor in physics was
a nightmare—she kept stopping to explain really basic
stuff to me just as if I couldn't keep up with the rest of
the class. Me! The one who audited that summer
physics class at the UW!
Holly and I sat together and she wrote me notes about
who everyone was. But the really exceptionally cool
thing was at lunch, Aidan was in line—gah, *queue*—for
the gack they served as food, and he told me to cut in.
Now you know there is nothing, *nothing* worse than
that feeling of going into a cafeteria when you don't
have anyone to sit with, and you don't know where the
cool spots are, and what the rules are, and stuff like

that. So when Aidan rescued me from certain lunchtime hell, I could have kissed him. Hahahahahah!

We had lunch together, him and some of his sixth form friends. At last, I was with my own kind! And they were nice, too, not like the nasty fifth formers. I wanted Holly to come with us, but she slipped off and sat at the end of a table by herself. It made me feel very bad, let me tell you. I'm going to tell her tomorrow she has to eat lunch with me and the hip guys. It will do her good.

Aidan . . . what can I say about him—he is the perfect Mr. Emily. He introduced me to Peg and a ditzy redhead named Lalla. Ditzy, but nice. Peg I'm pretty sure is a lesbian. She talks really fast and laughs very loud, and she wore her tie tied up really tight under her collar, not loose like the rest of the girls (they made me un-bow-tie mine). She was nice as well, and we all chatted about stuff, and they felt really bad that I was stuck in the fifth form with a bunch of brats who were so nasty.

ITC was great, although these people have a lot to learn about Net savvy. Honestly, the school Web site is positively archaic! I told one of the IT teachers, Miss Ryan, that I worked on our school's Web page, and had done an online class in web design this summer, so she signed me up to work on revamping the Web page, which will count as part of my ITC work. Very cool! I think I'm going to try to set up a chat room for the students. You know how much fun we had in last year's chat room.

And now what you're waiting to hear—the French class. I thought the stupid schedule they'd given me was wrong or something, but I went to the class anyway. I figured I'd tell the teacher that I'd never had

French, that I took Spanish at our school, but I didn't even have a chance to open my mouth. I walked into the class, and whammo! I was hit with a wall of French.

"*Beaucoup merci* frog legs, escargot?" the teacher asked me, pointing to a chair. The two evil Snickerers (as I have named them) sat in the front row and immediately started snickering as I stood there trying to decide what to do.

That was pretty much all it took—I decided right then and there that I would not give them anything more to snicker at, so I just nodded my head and said, "*Gracias. I mean, merci*," and took the seat the teacher was pointing to. Snickerer Ann leaned over and rattled off a mouthful of French at me, then laughed when I didn't respond. Honestly Dru, it's bad enough to have people be mean to you when you can understand them, but when you don't even know what it is they're saying about you—gah!

I ground my teeth (again) and swore not to let them see that I cared what they said (again). And as for French . . . well, I knew that sooner or later the teacher would find out that I didn't speak French, but until then, I would be über-coolio Emily and pretend nothing was the matter.

Get this—there was not one single word of English spoken during the whole class! I thought England hated France? Every time the teacher came around to talk to me, I had to pretend I had something in my throat and hacked and coughed and wheezed until she (I have no idea of her name, I think it's Madame Garcon or something) moved on to the next person. So I spent the whole of the class pretending that I understood, nodding, and saying, "*Oui, oui!*" a lot.

Aidan told me later that French is compulsory here, which just thrills me to death. NOT! How on earth am I supposed to pass a class of French when everyone in there has been speaking it since they were an embryo? I refuse to let my GPA drop because of this stupid school!

There, that's it, that's everything. It was the worst day of my life, and to top everything off, one of the Snickerers (Bee) saw me get into the car when Mom picked me up, which I'm sure she'll tell everyone.

Please e-mail me as soon as you get this. I'm going to go get my personally autographed picture of Oded and set it on top of the computer. Oded can conquer even the worst horrible day.

Hugs and kisses,
~Em

Subject: Re: WHAT????????????
From: Mrs.Oded@btelecom.co.uk
To: Dru@seattlegrrl.com
Date: 8 September 2003 11:14 pm

Dru wrote:
> What do you mean, Vance was driving Tabitha around
> last night? What do you know?

Um. My mistake. I . . . um . . . thought you said he drove Tabitha to the mall and went to Red Robin later. But I must have hallucinated that.

Hugs and kisses,
~Em

Subject: Re: OHMIGOD! He was with TABITHA?
From: Mrs.Oded@btelecom.co.uk
To: Dru@seattlegrrl.com
Date: 8 September 2003 11:19 pm

Dru wrote:
> THEY WENT TO RED ROBIN? Together? LIKE ON A
> DATE??? AAAaaaaaaaaaaaaaaaaaaaaaaaaaaargh!

   Honestly, how would I know what they did? I'm halfway around the world, for Pete's sake! Get a grip, girlfriend!

   Hs & Ks,
   ~Em

Subject: Re: I am never speaking to you again!
From: Mrs.Oded@btelecom.co.uk
To: Dru@seattlegrrl.com
Date: 8 September 2003 11:23 pm

Dru wrote:
> Did she tell you she and Vance had a date? What
> else did they do? Oh, God, I can't believe this! She
> e-mailed you EVERYTHING! My life is over! You owe
> it to me, as your very best friend, to tell me the
> truth. Did that b*tch Tabitha e-mail you?

   Um . . . maybe.

   Big, big hug (you deserve better than him),
   ~Em

Subject: The OTP must go!
From: Mrs.Oded@btelecom.co.uk
To: Dru@seattlegrrl.com
Date: 12 September 2003 5:21 pm

If it's the last thing I do, I'm going to get that Karen Duff! She told old Horseface, who told Mr. "Russell Crowe Near Miss" Krigon, that I said the policy of wearing the stupid games skirt for hockey was obviously the creation of a perverted mind. I can't believe she ratted on me! Aidan told me I could study with him in the library, but instead I had to spend my entire study period sweeping up the girls' locker room!

She's history. Oh, yes, she's history. Hiiiiiiiiiiiistory!

Hugs and smooches,
~Em

Subject: My fifteen minutes of fame . . . can I ask for my money back?
From: Mrs.Oded@btelecom.co.uk
To: Dru@seattlegrrl.com
Date: 16 September 2003 5:08 pm

"So," I said to Brother when he strolled in the door this afternoon (the man hardly works! It's terrible the way he gets paid for doing nothing but writing a few papers and teaching a couple of classes). "Would you like to explain this?"

He raised his Unibrow (still no signs of plucking, but I'm not giving up hope. I put Mom's extra pair of tweezers on his pillow. Maybe they'll get kinky and she'll pluck his Unibrow for him). "You seem to misunderstand the basic principles behind the parent-child relationship. Traditionally it is the parent who asks for an explanation of the child."

"Let's keep our mind in this century, shall we?" I asked, and held out the newspaper that Mom had given me.

He took it and read. "Ah. How nice. Very flattering. Hmmm. Noted medieval scholar, distinguished lecturer, mmmm. Yes. Very nice. I had no idea the university would notify the local papers."

"You are missing the important part." I pointed to the sentences in question.

"'Professor and Mrs. Williams are accompanied by their two daughters, Bess and Emily. The former, eighteen, will be studying at the Guildston Art Studio, while the latter, sixteen, will be a student in the fifth form at Piddlington-on-the-Weld's own Gobottle School.' What's wrong with that?"

"Gah! Brother! Can't you read? It says right there in black and white that I'm in the fifth form!"

"You are."

"But I shouldn't be. All of Aidan's friends agree about that!"

"Aidan?" Brother lowered the newspaper and gave me that *Have you been in the proximity of a male of the species?* look. You know, the one he always gives me when I go out on a date, the one that Mark Dickenson said made his noogies feel like they were being crushed in a vise.

"Aidan Spencer, the dean's son. He came here, remember?"

Bess walked by, a hideous plant in her arms, and a *Save the Bottle-nosed Dolphin* sign tucked into the back of her jeans. "Emily's got a boyfriend, Emily's got a boyfriend."

"You can stuff your plant where the dolphin don't shine," I told her. She grinned and went out to the kitchen.

"Oh, him," Brother said. "Nice boy. Polite. What about him?"

Honest to Pete, Dru, my father would get on a saint's nerves! How I'm going to live down having it blared to everyone in POTW that I'm in the fifth form, I'll never know. Just add it to the big old stack of stuff I have to bear.

Speaking of that, I had to pretend I was practicing to be a mime in French today. I even wrote up a little note for Madame Grayson saying I wasn't allowed to speak. She gave me an odd look, but so far so good. E-mail me that list of throat diseases you said you saw in the encyclopedia, would you?

Dru wrote:
> *don't think that it's like that. I mean, he did*
> *apologize, and the thing with Tabitha was totally a*
> *misunderstanding. Vance said he felt sorry for her*
> *because she had been dumped by George (the senior*
> *with the hunchback). Wouldn't you feel awful if you*
> *were dumped by a hunchback? I think Vance was*
> *being awfully nice to feel so sorry for her.*

Um. OK. If you're comfortable with him taking another girl out when you're stuck at home with a bum leg and nothing to do but watch *Survivor* with your mom and her boyfriend, well, it's not up to me to point out that HE IS A TWO-TIMING RAT FINK! So I won't. But I'm here for you if you need me.

So let me tell you about what happened at lunch. I was with the gang (Aidan and Peg and Lalla and Holly) and Aidan asks, in this really nonchalant Mr. Coolio way, if I've heard of anyone talking about the Polo Club.

I, of course, immediately go into shock because I know that this is it, after all these endless, long, never-ending days of waiting, he's going to ask me out on a real, honest to Pete date. But I must maintain the Emily cool, so I poke a bit of the ghastly dregs of preformed animal flesh they serve here as food into my mouth, and look like I'm thinking his question over.

"Why, no, I haven't. Is there something über-fabu about the Polo Club?"

He laughed and put his hand on mine and squeezed my fingers. All of them! I almost peed my pants. "Well, on Fridays they have local bands. I thought you might like to have a night out. Everyone will be there—Digger and Fang and Devon and the lot."

Digger is Lalla's boyfriend. He is the same age as Fang, and he works in a car-repair shop.

"Oooh, yes, do come with us," Lalla squealed. She's always squealing, but I don't hold that against her. "Digger's cousin's sister's boyfriend is in the band that's playing this week. The Count Dreadfuls. They're very, very rad."

I think that meant they were cool beans.

"Oh, sure, I'd"—Love. Be on my knees with gratitude. Swoon into your arms—"like to go."

"Great," Aidan said, pulling his hand from mine to pick up a limp French fry. "I'll pick you up round eight, then?"

"Sure," I said again. Yes, yes, no bonus points for verbal skills, but I defy anyone to be able to trip the tongue fantastic with Aidan holding her hand.

So now I have to use the next four days to decide what I'm going to wear on this Most Important Date. I really want to wear my slinky red dress, the one that looks like it was painted on, but when I tried it on this afternoon, I found out a horrible thing has happened.

My butt has expanded.

I think it has something to do with the change in hemispheres or being close to the Greenwich time thingy, or maybe it's the ghost (update on the undie ghost—the duct tape worked beautifully, thank you! I dare any ghost to fondle my bras while a web of duct tape is holding the drawer closed). I don't know what it is, but it's a terrible tragedy. So now I have to diet my butt like mad until Friday. Do you still have that issue of *Vogue* that has the butt exercises? If so, will you scan it and e-mail it to me? I'm doing cheek clenches every chance I get, but it's kind of hard to walk and clench at the same time. I tried when I came downstairs, and Mom asked me if I had to go to the bathroom.

And speaking of that (don't get grossed out, now) . . . I've been going to Gallbladder now for over a week, and I have *yet* to eat any recognizable food there. Oh, I try, I really try. Every day Holly and I march into the cafeteria. Every day she buys something to eat. Almost every day I end up with an apple or an orange and a package of cookies, which for some reason the Brits insist on calling "biscuits." Why the fruit-and-cookie diet, you ask? I'll tell you why. Here's what's been on the menu for the last couple of days:

Turkey Twizzlers or Gammon & Pineapple

Cheesy Wheels or Chicken Teddies
Fish Whales or Chicken Korma
Toad in the Hole or Chicken Jungles

Do you recognize anything on that list as being even remotely edible? I was there staring at them, and trust me, they aren't! I thought maybe it was just the school food, but Peg, who brings her lunch to school because she says the school food is loaded with sulfites and carcinogens and other things that Bess is always going on about, felt sorry for me yesterday.

"Like a bit of my butty?" she asked me as I ate my pathetic orange.

Now, you know I would never in any other circumstances eat someone else's food, but I was starving.

"Thanks, that would be cool. If you don't mind. It's just that lunch today . . . I mean, what exactly *is* a chicken jungle?"

She laughed, Lalla laughed, Aidan (who was eating a toad in the hole, which, I guess, is explained by the fact that England is so close to France—you know, they eat frog's legs there) laughed, everyone laughed but Holly, who was chewing on a jungle.

"Here you go," Peg said as she handed me half a sandwich. I took it and gave it a good, close look (if it had sprouts on it, I'd have to pick them out. You know how sprouts make me gag). There were no sprouts, but honest to Pete, I didn't recognize what was in the sandwich.

"Thanks," I said politely (bonus points for manners). "Um . . . what kind of butty is this?"

"Marmite," she said kind of indistinctly, her mouth being full of butty.

"Marmite? Isn't that some sort of monkey that lives in Madagascar or somewhere?" EW! Even if the man of my dreams, the future Mr. Emily, was at that very moment consuming a toad, I *was* not going to eat a monkey sandwich! There is a limit to how far I'm willing to go for love!

Bits of Marmite butty spewed out of her mouth as Peg choked. "No, those are marmosets. Marmite is a savory."

I looked at it, decided that something called a savory couldn't be that bad, and took a bite.

I was *so* wrong.

Ten minutes later, after I'd come back from gagging into the nearest girls' lav and brushing my teeth three times in a row (and my tongue five times), I sank back down into the chair in the caf. "What on earth is *in* that stuff?" I asked.

Aidan gave me another one of those adorable grins and a wink. "Marmite is yeast extract."

"YEAST!" I yelled, staring in horror at Peg. "You're eating a yeast sandwich?"

"It's very healthy," she said, opening a bag of shrimp-flavored potato chips, which are gacky enough, but they're no yeast extract.

"Yeah, well, cod-liver oil is healthy—that doesn't mean I want to make a milkshake out of it. Yeast!"

"Extract," Aidan added. "It's basically what's leftover after beer is brewed."

"Leftover?" I asked. "You mean like *sludge?*"

"Healthy sludge," Peg said.

"Dead grotty," Lalla murmured.

"I can't believe you offered me a dead grotty sludge butty," I told Peg. "I realize I'm American and all, and used to really good coffee and fresh salmon and stuff, but is that any reason to knowingly feed me beer sludge?"

She rolled her eyes and offered a carrot stick.

"What's that?" I asked suspiciously.

"Carrot, silly."

I eyeballed it. "Is it coated in roofing tar? Chum? Something else that is banned by the UN for being toxic, but which you think is healthy?"

She laughed again. "It's just a carrot stick."

"Marmite isn't for everyone," Aidan said as he scarfed down the last of his toad. "It's an acquired taste."

Yeah, right, like eating amphibians?

Update: Mom just told me that toad in the hole doesn't actually have any toad in it. It's really sausages deep fried in a batter or something. If that's the case, why do they call it toad? I don't quite buy it. Any country that sells yeast sludge as a sandwich spread wouldn't think twice about putting real toads in their holes.

Gotta run, din-din time. Oh, hey, before I forget, what happened to SimTabitha? Did she drink the poisoned absinthe? Did you plead with the Grim Reaper for her? I sent SimEmily downtown on a date with Simon Townie (the one with the pierced nose and perpetual shades) and the creep dumped her! After she paid for a nice dinner and everything! And she was looking über-hot, too.

Fill me up with news, girl!

Hugs and kisses,
~Em

Subject: He is Slicker than Snot on a Doorknob!
From: Mrs.Oded@btelecom.co.uk
To: Dru@seattlegrrl.com
Date: 18 September 2003 9:19 pm

Dru wrote:
> what am I going to do, tell him he's lying? Of course
> I'm not! And I know him, Em, much better than you
> do. He'd never two-time me like that, especially with
> Tabitha the Hun. So stop worrying and tell me what
> you're going to wear on Friday.

Ha! It's easy for you to tell me to stop worrying, but you don't see your best friend making the *biggest* mistake of her life. I'm warning you, Dru— Oh, poop, never mind. I can tell you're not going to pay attention to anything I say. Fine. I'll just wait around keeping my thoughts (he's a grade-A mimbo) to myself. When you want me to pick up the pieces of what remains of your life after he's trampled all over you, just let me know.

Tomorrow . . . well, those butt exercises don't seem to be helping much. I clench and do the pelvic thrusts whenever no one is looking, but I think Mr. Thorpe (he's one of the IT teachers, not much to look at, but the man's a whiz at figuring out what's wrong with my JavaScripts) noticed me doing them. He came over when I was working on getting the chat room set up, and asked me if there was something wrong with the chair I was sitting on.

"Something wrong?" I asked, mortified. I mean, really! He probably thought I had my underwear stuck up my butt or something. It was totally embarrassing.

"You don't seem to be very comfortable."

I blinked and smiled and showed a lot of teeth and prayed he wouldn't notice I was blushing like mad. "The chair's fine. No problems."

"Ah. How is the update to the Web site coming?"

"Peachy keen. Holly is working on the calendar and school news, and all I have left to do is update the staff bios."

"Excellent. Good work, Emily." He smiled, then got a really odd look on his face. "And . . . erm . . . if you need to spend a penny, don't feel you need to ask my permission."

Dru, I almost died right there and then. "Spend a penny" is another one of those weirdo English phrases, but this one means to pee! He told me I could pee if I had to! He thought I had to pee! What is this pee fixation the Brits have? Spend a penny, Piddlington-on-the-wee, Marmite . . . well, OK, Marmite doesn't have anything to do directly with peeing, but it comes from beer leftovers, and everyone knows beer makes you pee a lot!

Sometimes I think I'll never live through this year.

Good news on the vengeance front: the English Lit teacher (who yells everything—her name is Mrs. Spreadborough, and no, I'm not kidding) is the head of the fifth form, and she came up to me yesterday. I thought it was because OTP Duff had been trying to make more trouble for me. You're not going to believe this, but the Duff turned Holly and me in for using the tennis court on our study period. Yeah, OK, so we were, but is that the end of the world?

I told Mr. Krigon, "My father always says that half of studying is mentally digesting the work, and we were digesting while we were having a quick game. Exercise promotes brain stuff, you know."

He didn't buy that. We both swept out the girls' locker room.

Anyway, Mrs. Spread pulled me aside after class and told me she had a project for me. Actually, she bellowed it at me, and I made a mental note to leave some hearing aid pamphlets in her mailbox.

"I HAVE A LITTLE PROJECT I THINK YOU MIGHT LIKE, WILLIAMS," she screamed. "I KNOW HOW YOU YANKS LIKE HALLOWEEN, SO I'M PUTTING YOU IN CHARGE OF THIS YEAR'S HALLOWEEN PARTY."

Now, my first thought was, *No way, José*, but then I started thinking about it. Who puts on the coolest parties at North Seattle High? Well, OK, it's you, but I'm the one who helps you! What the Spreadable said next really clinched it for me.

"SEE MISS DARLING IN THE OFFICE FOR INFORMATION ON THE BUDGET. YOU MAY ORGANIZE A TEAM OF VOLUNTEERS FROM THE FIFTH FORM."

You see where my evil thoughts are going, don't you? Heh heh heh. Oh, yes, I'll organize a team of volunteers, and I know one Miss Karen Duff who'll be given the worst, the most grungy, filthily repulsive job I can find. Then we'll see who goes tattling to Mr. Krigon every friggin' day!

I could get used to this revenge stuff.

Oh, the underwear ghost has struck again. When I went to my room today after school, my undies were all over the floor. There was a bra *on top* of the wardrobe, but—and this is so weird—the duct tape was still Xed tight across the front of the drawer! Isn't that creepy? I'm starting to think it's either Mom or Brother doing it, and if it is, I really hope it's Mom, cause if it's Brother fondling my things, I'm *really* going to freak out.

So you asked about tomorrow night, the Coolio Big Datio. Well, since all the clenching and thrusting doesn't seem to have made much of a difference to my butt, I've decided to wear my black-and-pink slashed tiger fishnet dress. I know you think it makes me look like a rocker chick, but the diagonal stripes do a really good job of hiding the problem with my butt. I'm going to wear that and a long pink ribbon as a choker, and, of course, the stilettos. This is a very important date, so I have to look taller, because everyone knows taller looks more mature. Do you think I should go with fishnet or lace nylons? Will fishnet with fishnet be too much? What am I saying? Can you ever have too much fishnet? I think not. Guys like fishnets. They think they're sexy (which is stupid, because if they ever wore them they'd know that all they do is rub your thighs raw).

Oh, I forgot to answer you the other day—I'm reading Dr. Ruth. She has a section on how to get a guy excited and stuff. Bess came in while I was reading it, and told me I should practice on a carrot, which is so embarrassing! It's bad enough I have to read Dr. Ruth to find out how to do these things, I don't need my older sister telling me how to arouse a carrot!

I think something's wrong with my Sims. SimEmily is ralphing all over the place, and slapping anyone who comes to her house. She even yelled at her husband, SimOded, and you *know* that SimEmily never yells at SimOded! Ever! Not even when he was gettin' it on with SimSamantha, the woman who lives next door and likes to sit in her hot tub naked during the middle of the day. I wonder if there's a Sim virus going around. Are your Sims OK? Let me know.

E-mail me ASAP. I promise I won't lecture you any more about dumping Vance, or setting his hair on fire, or suggesting you tattoo "LOSER" on his forehead. I'll just keep those thoughts to myself.

Hugs and kisses,
~Em

Subject: Just a quickie
From: Mrs.Oded@btelecom.co.uk
To: Dru@seattlegrrl.com
Date: 19 September 2003 7:22 pm

Visualize the girl: pink-and-black dress in alternating panels of fishnet and nylon. Black stilettos (have to stuff them in my bag because Brother will come unglued if he sees them). Fishnets. Pink ribbon dripping down my back like . . . um . . . something really pink. Hair back in black-and-pink scrunchy. Glitter on the upper boobs. Makeup: Riotous Red lipstick, Raisin and Nickel eye shadow, Omber Rose blush, kohl for eyeliner, indigo mascara. I am coolio personified!

Details after the Big D!

Hugs and kisses,
~Em

Subject: Just a quickie, part 2
From: Mrs.Oded@btelecom.co.uk
To: Dru@seattlegrrl.com
Date: 19 September 2003 7:48 pm

CRAP! Mister Monthly Visitor is here! No wonder my butt is huge! Why now? Why tonight? WHY WHY WHY???

H&K
~Emily of the cramps

Subject: Tell me what you think
From: Mrs.Oded@btelecom.co.uk
To: Dru@seattlegrrl.com
Date: 20 September 2003 11:50 am

This is going to be a really long e-mail, so you may want to go to the bathroom now. I have a ton to tell you, and I don't want you squirming around in your chair because you've been drinking diet Coke all morning and your crutches fell too far away from you or whatever, and now you have to go and you can't. Hey, speaking of that, when do you get the walking cast? And are they going to take the pins out of your ankle?

All right, now for the dirt. As you know, last night was the Big Date. Everything started out mondo cool, except Bess ratted on me to Brother about the stilettos, so I had to wear my platform SIN shoes instead. They were OK for the first couple of hours, but after that my feet really started hurting. I'm going to try and find a new pair here because I just CAN'T go out without platforms!

Aidan, looking hunkalicious in black, showed up with his dad's car. Brother insisted on doing the father thing and grilled him about the date.

"Emily has to be back by one," he said once Aidan explained about the club. "I will remind you that she is only sixteen, and neither her mother nor I want her drinking."

"Brother, you are *so* embarrassing me!" I hissed, and tugged on Aidan's sleeve to get him away from the horrible man who spawned me.

"If you plan on drinking, you are not to drive Emily home."

GAH!

"Don't worry about Emily, sir. I'll take good care of her."

Poor Aidan, driven to say "sir" by the ramblings of a deranged, tyrannical father.

Brother narrowed his eyes at Aidan, the Unibrow and hair horn making him look even more than normal like a rhinoceros. "And no sex! I absolutely forbid any sort of sex! She's too young."

"BRO-*THER!*" I prayed for the earth to open right up and swallow me, but it didn't. Then I prayed for it to swallow Brother, but when are my prayers ever answered?

Aidan gave Brother a kind of strained smile. "Mr. Williams, I—"

"Nothing. No inappropriate touching, nothing. You understand me?"

I thought lovingly of the roll of duct tape up in my room, and how much I'd like to see it across my father's face at that moment.

"I respect Emily, sir," Aidan said, all righteous and gentlemanly and really, really fabu. "I would never dishonor her."

I groaned and sat down on the hall bench. You know what the word "honor" does to my medieval-minded father.

"It's a good thing you mentioned honor," Brother said, and went into a ten-minute spiel of how ye olde knights of yore honored women, and what was wrong with society today that couldn't be fixed by a wallop upside the head with a sword or two. I think that's what he was going on about—I really wasn't paying too much attention. Instead I was wondering exactly how you draw and quarter someone, and whether it would be enough to SHUT BROTHER UP.

Honestly, I could have killed him right then and there, but Aidan would probably think the worst of me, so I didn't. I figured I'd kill him after I came home.

We finally escaped. I apologized all the way to the Polo Club, but Aidan, who was the absolute most perfect man, just laughed and told me his father is worse with his sisters.

The Polo Club was on the other side of POTW. I don't know what it has to do with polo, 'cause the place is in the basement of a warehouse. There's, like, a million steps down to it, and the floor is cement (which is probably why my feet hurt), and there's big steel girders with Christmas lights wrapped around them every twenty feet or so, and exposed pipes, and the place smells like rusty pond water.

In other words, it was completely über-coolio.

It was really packed, lots of people, music from a CD booming away while the band was setting up, and everyone was dancing, dancing, dancing. Aidan grabbed my hand and dragged me to the rear, where a bunch of round tables and those little white plastic chairs people have on their patios were set up.

"There's the lads," he said, and hauled me over to where Fang and Devon were. Devon had two girls with him: a redhead with her hair spiked out stood behind him rubbing his shoulders, and a blonde with long poofy hair (it must take a whole bottle of hair spray to get it looking like that) who was rubbing her hand up and down his leg. Even so, he grinned at me and winked, and did a little wolf whistle when he looked over the slashed tiger fishnet dress. I thought about giving him the Slitted-eye Look of Pure Scorn for flirting with me when there were two other girls practically slobbering on him, but decided I'd better not. He was very hot in leather pants and a kind of see-through red shirt, and he had a tattoo of a dragon coiled around his left arm, and you *know* how I love tats!

I sat next to Fang, who smiled and asked me how school was going. I chatted with him for a bit when Aidan left to get us some drinks. When he came back, he had two of those big pints of beer, one of which he plopped down in front of me. Now you know me, Dru—I'm not totally unhip when it comes to drinks, but it did kind of take me by surprise. I mean, he'd just promised Brother that he wasn't going to drink and drive, and yet here he was chugging back a big old pint of beer. I know I'm going to sound like an awful twit, but it made me kind of uncomfortable. I mean, I trusted Aidan, I really did, but it still made me feel a little weird.

But everyone else had beer, so I figured I'd just sip mine (I don't know what people see in the stuff. It isn't nearly as good as those Mai Tais you and I made during the summer when your mom was in Aspen). Aidan sat really close to me and put his arm around me, which made me go all girly inside, but at the same time, I was a bit worried. If he was drinking when he told Brother he wouldn't be drinking, did that mean he'd want to have sex, too? And if he did want to, what was I going to do about it?

The band got started just about the time I was trying to decide if I would tell him a little touching was as far as I was going to go. Devon, who had been snogging the poofy blonde (snogging means French kissing), got up and went off with *both* girls to the dance floor.

Fang laughed when he saw the surprise on my face. "Our Dev's quite the lad with the ladies."

"I guess," I said, watching the three of them dance together. "I've heard of a *ménage à trois*, but I've never seen one before."

Fang choked and shot beer out of his nose. Poor guy, I have to admit I felt a bit sorry for him then. There we were, Devon with two girls, Aidan with me, and Fang had no one, and now he'd just spewed in front of us. I helped him mop up, and decided that I'd make sure to dance with him at least once, and wondered who I know who might want to date him. He was a nice guy, he really was, even if he was quiet. I was wondering if he'd like Bess when he got up to go wipe the beer off his pants.

"You've been awful quiet tonight, duck," Aidan whispered after Fang left, and trailed his tongue right around the edges of my ear. Now, I told you that Mark D. and I got a bit busy that night we went to Lilith Fair, right? Well, Mark did the same thing, but the way Aidan did it kind of made me melt into a puddle. I decided it would be cool for me to kiss him back, so I was just making kissy lips to do it, when all of a sudden he grabbed my hand and dragged it over toward his . . . you know. *Thingie!* I was so shocked that my hand kind of jerked back right at the last moment, and ended up on his thigh. ON HIS THIGH! I didn't know what to do—if I took my hand away, he would think I didn't like either him or his thigh, and I did, I liked both. But if I left my hand there . . . well, he might think that I really wanted to touch him . . . *there* . . . and, well, OK, to be honest, I didn't.

I know, I know. We've talked about this sort of a situation, and read about it, and honest, up to the point that Aidan grabbed my hand and tried to make me touch his thingie, I thought I wanted it . . . but sometimes, Dru, things just aren't what you imagined them to be! I thought it was going to be, you know, like in the books and stuff, but it wasn't, it was . . . *weird!*

Aidan started kissing my neck, and I sat there feeling like a raving idiot, my hand on his thigh, kind of panting because I'd sucked all the air out of the room a minute before so there wasn't any oxygen left, and wondering what he was going to do next, and then he did it! His mouth swooped down on mine for a kiss, AND THEN HIS TONGUE TOUCHED MY LIPS! It wasn't gross or anything, but it was definitely *tonguey* and it made me jump straight up, which ended up with me smashing my chin into his nose. Hard.

"Bloody hell," he snarled as he jerked back, holding his face and glaring at me. "What the hell is the matter with you?"

"Oh, God, I'm so sorry," I said, then felt my jaw drop when he pulled his hand away from his nose. It was covered with blood. I'd mortally wounded him! When he was trying to *French kiss me!* While I had my hand on his thigh! "I just . . . I didn't expect . . . you kind of startled me . . . "

"I thought you wanted me to. You've been giving me the signals for the last couple of weeks."

Signals? There're signals? Why didn't anyone tell me that?

"I do want you to, I just . . . you just . . . it's . . . it's . . . "

He muttered something that sounded like "stupid bird." I realized I was still holding on to his leg, and jerked my hand back, then started fumbling around in my purse for a tissue, blinking furiously to beat back the tears. Before I could give him the tissues, Fang came back.

"Nosebleed?" was all he said. He handed Aidan a handful of napkins and gave me a long look as Aidan muttered something about getting some water. He went off to the men's room and left me sitting there feeling like the stupidest idiot in the whole, wide world. Honestly, Dru, have you ever known anyone so cursed as me? Ever since I met Aidan, I've waited for this moment, and all I did was freeze up and pant and probably broke his nose. I wanted to cry so badly, but I couldn't because Fang was there and it would have been too embarrassing to have him know what an *idiot* I am.

"All right?" Fang asked. I nodded, but couldn't look at him, because then he'd see that I was fighting back tears.

"I know I'm not who you fancy, but would you like to dance?"

I almost burst into tears at that point, but we Williamses are made of pretty heavy-duty stuff, so instead I swallowed back the tears and nodded again. Fang took my hand and led me out to the dance floor. I tried to concentrate on Fang, because I've always felt it's only polite to think about the person you're dancing with, but I couldn't help wondering about poor Aidan and what he must have thought of me. He probably thought it was a good idea I was back in the fifth form with all the babies.

I decided right then and there that I would prove to Aidan that I wasn't really an idiot who jumped just because he licked my lips. If he wanted to do the Deed, then I would. I think. Maybe. Or not. Oh, I don't know anymore! Everything is so different than what I thought it was going to be like!

I danced with Fang some more, and when the song was over, we went back to the table. On the way there, he pulled me aside for a second.

"You don't have to do anything you don't want to do," he said, looking me straight in the eye. "Don't let Aidan push you into something you're not ready for."

I blushed about a thousand-degree blush and looked away. How did he know what I was thinking? How did he know I was thinking about doing it with Aidan? My God, did everyone know? I didn't say anything. I mean, what could I say? To a guy? GAH!

When we got back to the table, Aidan was there, with Devon and his two girls . . . and Tash. She was leaning into Aidan, whispering to him. His eyes were on me, but he was whispering right back at her, and then she laughed. I wanted to die right then. I knew they were talking about me. No doubt he was telling her what a childish baby I was over a little kissing and thigh holding.

The rest of the evening pretty much sucked. Aidan danced with me three times, and I danced with Devon (without his two chicks) twice, but I could tell that Aidan was disappointed with me. I mean, it was pretty obvious. He didn't even try to kiss me again.

"Last drink for me, mate," Aidan said later when Devon came back with another round of pints. "I promised Emily's dad I'd have her back safe and sound by one."

Oh, right, like I wasn't humiliated enough, he had to tell everyone I had a curfew? ACK! I tried to slouch under the table, but there wasn't enough room what with everyone's legs.

"Really? Do you turn into a pumpkin if you're out too late?" Tash asked with her barracuda smile. I thought about telling her she had something green stuck in her teeth, then decided not to. It would serve her right to go around with food in her teeth and not know it.

"Oh, you know, it's just my father. I don't really have to be back right at one."

"When was the last time you had a curfew, Linda?" Tash asked. Linda was the poofy-haired blonde. She stopped picking her nails (the redhead was dancing with Devon) and looked up.

"My mum doesn't care when I'm home, as long as I don't wake her when I come in."

Tash smiled again, another really mean smile. They ought to put her out in cornfields. I bet the crows would take one look at her smile and drop down dead. "Well, I haven't had one since I was fourteen. I guess it's all to do with how mature one is."

I kind of hoped Aidan would say something in my defense, but all he did was finger the bridge of his nose and smile at Tash. And it was all my fault! I almost had him and then I had to screw it all up!

"I think it's a nice change," Fang suddenly said. I told you he was really quiet, right? He is. I think he's shy. The guys ribbed him a lot about being there without a girl, but he just smiled and took it all.

"What is?" Tash asked.

"A father who cares enough about his daughter that he wants her home before anything can happen to her."

Fang gave me an odd kind of look that sent me slumping down in my chair with the realization that he felt sorry for me. ME! Honest to Pete, Dru, I've never been so miserable in my life. Here I was feeling sorry for Fang because he didn't have a girlfriend, and all along he was feeling sorry for me because I'm such a wet blanket. It was awful.

"Come along then, duck," Aidan said after he drained his pint. He stood up and kind of swayed, which made me even more miserable. You remember I told you that one of my cousins was killed when the guy she was riding with plowed into the freeway overpass? Vicki was sixteen then (this was like five years ago)—just our age now! After that, I promised Mom and Brother that I'd never ride with anyone who was drunk, and yet here I was going to ride home with Aidan. I'm not saying he was sloshed or anything, but he weaved a bit as we said good-bye to everyone.

I was sure Tash was going to make a stink, or offer to come with us or something, but she didn't. She just smiled and looked like the cat who'd eaten all the cream. "Come back as soon as you're done taking Cinderella home, love."

Aidan inclined his head in what could be a nod, or he could have been giving her a look that told her he'd rather be eaten alive by fire ants than hang out with her. I couldn't see, his back was to me, but after the kiss/nose episode, I was willing to bet it was the first.

I wanted to die.

"Godda bleed the sausage," he said as we got to the top of the stairs. There were bathrooms up there as well as in the club itself, but these were down a long, cold hallway, so everyone used the downstairs bathrooms. "Stay here. Be out inna tick."

He went into the men's room. I dashed into the ladies' to make sure I didn't have lipstick on my teeth (just in case he felt like giving me a good night kiss, not that I thought he would because by now he was convinced I was just a child), and scooted back out to the empty hallway to wait for him. There was a draft blowing bits of paper and stuff around the floor, and although I could still hear the sound of the music from the club downstairs, the upper floor was quiet. Eerily quiet.

Aidan came out of the bathroom. He didn't look pissed at me, which was good, but he wasn't walking quite right, which was bad. I didn't want to get killed if he drove us home, but I absolutely could *not* take the embarrassment of telling him I wouldn't ride home with him because he was snockered. I just stood there like a boob, trying to think of a nice way to suggest calling Brother.

Suddenly Aidan pushed me up against the cold cement brick wall, his breath hot on my face. He smelled like beer and breath mints (not a thrilling combination, I can tell you). I gasped in surprise when his hands kind of skimmed my body as he leaned into me.

"Oh, baby," he said. The way he said "baby" would have melted me into a puddle under normal circum-stances, but this was a little too weird. I was thrilled that he had changed his mind and wanted to kiss me again, but I wasn't sure if it was all the beer he'd drunk, or if he really did want me.

"Um . . . Aidan . . . " His fingers were heading straight for my boobs, which made me even more nervous. Part of me wanted to let him touch my boobs, but the other part of me just wanted to get out of there. I felt kind of trapped what with him leaning on me, and breathing on me and all. "Um. Maybe this isn't such a good idea."

"What's wrong, duck? You want this, I know you do. I can tell by the way you've been looking at me." He kissed me then, and I have to say that although I really, really like Aidan—when he hasn't been drinking beer— I really didn't want him kissing me right there where anyone could see us. His lips were wet and . . . oh, it's hard to describe what was wrong. Maybe it was me, I don't know for sure, all I do know is that although I wanted to be with Aidan (I really did), I didn't really like his wet-lipped kiss.

I squirmed out from where he was holding me up against the wall. "Um . . . you know, I think maybe I should go home now."

He pulled back and gave me a weird look. "Little tease. The least you can do is take care of me."

"Take care of you?" Did that mean sex? Or a hand job? Or a BJ? Why doesn't someone publish a guide to this sort of thing so people like me know what's going on? It's hard being a sixteen-year-old virgin! I know it's really juvie to run away from things, but . . . well, that's kind of what I did. I couldn't help it, Aidan was freaking me out a bit. Oh, all right, it wasn't just a little freak-out, it was major huge panic time. "I really have to go now!"

He grabbed for me then, but I turned around and ran down the hallway to the doors. I know what you're thinking—what happened to wanting to do it with Aidan? All I can say is that there's a big, big difference in reading about sex and stuff, and having a real live guy right there in front of you, expecting you to do things with him!

Aidan snarled something I won't repeat here because I won't lower myself to having such a potty mouth, and followed after me. I tried to apologize, but he just gritted his teeth and grabbed my arm (hard! I have a bruise!) and hauled me over to the front door.

Just as we got there I decided that I really didn't want to ride home with him. Not because he wanted me to touch him and all, but because I know Aidan. He's not really like that. It had to be all the beer he'd drunk that had made him that way. And if he was that drunk, he was too drunk to drive. So I took a deep breath and stopped just before he opened the door.

"I'm sorry, Aidan, but I don't think it's a good idea for you to be driving until you sober up a bit. I'll call my dad. He won't mind picking me up."

He stared at me for a minute, then said, "Suit yourself." Without another word he turned around and went back down the stairs to the club. Yes, I know I'd told him I'd have Brother get me, but I expected him to at least wait with me until then.

I have to admit, Dru, my faith in Aidan was a tiny bit shaken at that point. I knew it was just the beer making him act weird, but if he got like that on every date, I wasn't going to want to go out with him very often. And I wanted to, I really did. Which made it all really confusing.

I reached out for the door, but it swung back. Fang stood in the doorway, coming in from the outside. "Oh, hi," I said, feeling like an idiot for having jumped when the door opened.

"There you are. I was looking for you."

"For me? Why?"

He scratched his head. "Had an idea that Aidan was totally legless."

Oh, great, the worst night of my life, and I have to try to decipher more Englishisms. "Legless?"

"Pissed. Drunk."

"Oh. Yeah, he was a bit, so I told him I'd catch a ride with my dad."

Fang held the door open for me (which was really cool) and turned to walk with me as I headed for the front of the building where the pay phones were. "I'll take you home if you like."

I stopped and turned to glare at him. I *hate* being pitied! "Oh, really? What if you're just as legless as Aidan? You'll probably kiss me and shove your tongue into my mouth, too. You know, I think I've been propositioned enough tonight, so I'll take myself home."

He frowned and put one finger under my chin to tip my head back. "I told you that you didn't have to do anything you didn't want to do."

I pushed his finger away. "I didn't, not that it's any of your business."

"Good girl." He just stood there looking at me for a second, then I turned and headed to the street. "I'm not legless, but I don't have a car, so I won't be able to drive you. I will, however, walk you home if you'd rather not tell your dad."

It was the most I'd heard him say, and I checked it over carefully for obvious Pity Points, but it was pretty much pity-free. I really hated to let Brother know that Aidan had messed up and got drunk. The thought of the lectures he'd feel justified in giving me were enough to make me take Fang up on his offer. "That's awfully nice of you. Are you sure you don't mind?"

He took my hand in his (it was nice and warm) and started off down the street. "Bit of air will do me good."

So he walked me home. It was pretty cool, even though my feet hurt and it was getting cold out. Fang gave me his coat to wear, which was toasty from him and smelled like spicy aftershave, and never once complained when I stopped to let my feet rest. He even offered to carry me, which made me laugh and feel a bit better about the disastrous evening.

Fang whistled when we went up the drive to the Hell House. "That's some house."

"It's haunted," I said without thinking. Thank heaven it was dark out, so he couldn't see me blushing. I would die before I told him my underwear drawer was possessed!

"Is it? I wouldn't doubt it. Lots of ghosts in these parts." He said that really casually, as if it wasn't at all strange, which makes me wonder what they put in the water here.

He stopped at the bottom of the porch and I gave him back his coat. "Thanks, Fang, I really appreciate you coming home with me. My father is a professor, and he loves lecturing more than anything else. I would have had to sit through at least six hours if he found out that Aidan was too squiggly to drive."

He grinned. "I enjoyed it. Been a while since I walked a girl home."

Do you think that means he's gay? Maybe that's why he doesn't have a girlfriend. I gnawed on my lip for a couple of seconds until I decided I had to ask him (not whether he was gay, stupid!). "Um . . . is Fang your real name? I was just wondering if it was a nickname, and if so, why Fang? You don't have unusually long teeth or anything."

He laughed. "My real name is Francis."

I wrinkled up my nose. "Oh. That explains it. I don't blame you."

"Good night, Emily."

"Good night, Fang."

He put a hand on either arm and leaned forward until his lips just brushed mine. It was wonderful—until I realized exactly what it was.

A Pity Kiss.

That's it. My life is over. Not only have I turned down the perfect man when all he wanted was to get busy with me, I have sunk so low that I am now getting Pity Kisses.

Sorry this was so long. I'm going to go now. My back hurts (cramps) and I feel awful and I just want to curl up in my ghost-riddled room and pretend I'm back home where everyone thinks I'm cool and guys like me and no one gives me Pity Kisses.

E-mail me when you get up.

Hugs but no kisses, thank you,
~Em

Subject: Re: He didn't!
From: Mrs.Oded@btelecom.co.uk
To: Dru@seattlegrrl.com
Date: 20 September 2003 5:30 pm

Dru wrote:
> think he was wrong to just walk away and leave you
> at the door like that, but you know, you did give him
> a nosebleed. You know how guys are—they hate to
> look weak in front of us. So I think you should forgive
> him and see how he behaves at school. If he's cold to
> you, then screw him (not literally, of course). If he
> apologizes like he should, you can gracefully accept
> his apology and then you've got him by the short and
> curlies. It works with Vance!

Well, I ended up talking to Bess. You know how she's always yammering on about empowering my inner self and not letting boys treat me like a doormat and all that feminist stuff, which is OK, but this wasn't about that. At least I didn't think it was. Anway, it was her or Mom, and Mom is so old she just doesn't have a clue about what it's like to be our age. At least Bess was sixteen a couple of years ago. So anyway, Bess came in to borrow my red shawl, the one everyone loves, and she noticed me lying on my bed crying my eyes out.

"What's the matter, pipsqueak?" she asked as she rooted around in my wardrobe for my shawl. "Got dumped by your hottie date last night?"

I looked up from where I was sobbing into my Oded Fehr pillowcase (yes, I brought them, the whole set of six). "How did you know? Who told you? Does Brother know that Aidan was too drunk to drive me home, and French kissed me, and wanted me to do other things, but I didn't want to, and Fang walked me home and gave me a Pity Kiss?"

She blinked a couple of times, turned around really slowly, then closed the door to the hall and dragged a chair over to the bed. "Whoa, there. I was just teasing you, Em. No one told me anything, although if all that happened to you, I don't blame you for turning on the waterworks. You want to start at the top? Aidan got drunk? I thought he was only sixteen?"

"No, he's seventeen." I sniffled, and wiped my nose on Oded (I'll wash him later). "This club didn't seem to be too particular about who they sold beer to."

"Hmm. Did he try to drive home?"

"No, I told him I'd have Brother pick me up, so he said, 'Suit yourself,' and left me there."

"Was that before or after he slipped you the tongue?"

I sat up. "Geez, Bess, I'm not a hooker. It wasn't like that."

She raised both her eyebrows. If she doesn't watch out, she's going to have a Unibrow, too. "What was it like, then?"

I thought back to the cold hallway with Aidan kissing me with wet lips. "Well, he had this pouty look on his face like he thought he was being hot, only he wasn't because his lips were wet and slicky, and . . . and . . ." I started to snicker. "It was pretty funny, actually."

"Yeah, guys can be that way sometimes when they're trying to look sexy."

We looked at each other and started laughing. I laughed so hard I fell off the bed, which made Bess laugh even harder.

"See, you're feeling better already. OK, so what happened then? I take it you didn't let him do anything?"

"No. You don't think I should have, do you? He seemed awful mad at me afterward, but I just didn't think it was right then. Mom always said it should be with the right person at the right time, and I don't think standing in a freezing hallway is *right*."

"No, I think you did the right thing. First of all, no guy who really respects you is going to ask you to do anything on a first date. Second, he wasn't thinking about you at all. He probably just wanted to get his rocks off."

"Geez, Bess!" I said again, kind of embarrassed with her talking like that. I mean, my family aren't prudes, but here she was talking to me about sex and stuff like it was nothing! "I didn't say anything about having sex!"

She rolled her eyes. "Tell me about the rest of the evening. Who's this Fang when he's at home?"

I filled her in on the whole sorry night. "Hmm," she said again when I was through, then she stood up and went back to the wardrobe to pull out my red shawl. "Well, if you want my two cents, I think you were right to dump Aidan and go home with Fang. He sounds like a nice guy, and he obviously has the hots for you."

I stared at her. I don't know who she had been listening to for the last ten minutes, but it hadn't been me. "What, are the voices in your head talking again? Bess, I didn't dump Aidan, he dumped me. And Fang doesn't have the hots for me—he barely noticed me. He's just a nice guy who probably didn't want Aidan getting in trouble for driving when he was drunk."

"Uh-huh. Right. He was so worried about his friend that he left a club to walk all the way across town and go home alone. Sure." She leaned over and patted me on my cheek. "One day you're going to open your eyes and you'll see what sort of guy is really worth your time. Until then—don't let anyone push you into sex until you're ready."

Now she sounded just like Fang. Just what I needed—two of them giving me sexual advice.

"You know . . . " Bess stood in the middle of my room and tapped a finger on her chin. "I think you should come with me next weekend when I go to the Womyn's Festival and Celebration of Self. Monk's sister is holding an awareness hour at her house over in Alling. I think it would do you good."

I hugged Oded to my chest. "I've already told you my life is too messed up to go protest stuff."

"This isn't a protest, it's a festival of empowerment, to get in touch with your inner goddess."

"No blockades?" I asked her, suspicious. You know how she tricked us into going to that Greenpeace rally in Seattle, and we ended up with red paint on us from where they were throwing it on the gill-netters. "No paint or air horns or anything like that?"

"Just a bunch of women getting to know their deepest, innermost selves."

"Oh." That didn't sound too bad. They'd probably play some Sarah McLaughlin songs and light incense and meditate and stuff.

"You can bring your friend, the one with the rabbit teeth. What's her name?"

"Holly," I said, bristling a bit on Holly's behalf. She's only been over to the house once, but looked worried the whole time. "Yeah, she might like that. It would probably do her good."

"Do you both good." She threw one last piece of advice over her shoulder before she left. "If this Aidan has any feelings for you, he'll be on his knees groveling before you, apologizing for his behavior. If he doesn't, he's not worth it."

Oh, right! Like I can visualize Aidan on his knees apologizing for me being such a boob? Fwah!

Gotta run—it's dinner time—but I want to hear more about what you did to Connie that had Heidi shooting milk through her nose at lunch. E-mail me as soon as you get this. Sooner!

Hugs and kisses,
~Em (Oh, yeah, I forgot. I bought a mousetrap today and put it in my undie drawer. I'm going to get scientific about this ghost.)

Subject: You are just the coolest thing on one leg
From: Mrs.Oded@btelecom.co.uk
To: Dru@seattlegrrl.com
Date: 25 September 2003 6:18 pm

Dru wrote:
> Obviously he hasn't been at school because he's too
> embarrassed to face you. I'm with Bess on this: he
> owes you an apology, and if he doesn't give you one,
> you should dump him.

I don't have him to dump! No one knows what's happened to him. You can't die of a broken nose, can you? He's not answering his e-mail, and I'll die before I call his house. I did ask Peg and Lalla what they thought, but Lalla was too busy with her boyfriend last Friday to see anything that was happening at our table, and Peg didn't have any ideas about why Aidan was missing school. What should I do? Do you think I should go to his house? What if he refuses to see me? ACK! I'd die!

> Now, about your underwear ghost—that's too weird

> that you can't catch anyone at it. Have you looked at
> your parents' fingers closely? No signs that they are
> tripping the mousetrap?

None. I don't see how they can be setting off the trap, but almost every day when I come home, my under-wear is all over the place. I'm going to have to take the next step and coat the drawer handle with itching pow-der or something.

> Mom wants to go up to Whistler, but I don't want to
> go. I mean, it's not like there's any snow, and even if
> there was, I just got my walking cast! I don't think I
> should be skiing! So I told her I'd stay home and invite
> Heidi over to stay with me. Only I'm not going to.

OHMIGOD! You're going to invite Vance? To stay with you for the weekend? Does that mean you're going to let him? YOU HAVE TO TELL ME EVERYTHING! OMG! This is so . . . so majorly big! What are you going to do? What are you going to wear? Are you going to let him seduce you, or do you want to seduce him? Do you want me to send you my erotic massage book? It's not like I'm going to get any use out of it at the rate I'm going, and to think I went to all the trouble of smug-gling it in. Tell me everything!

My news is a bit anticlimactic (ha!) compared to yours. We had our first hockey practice today (we've been doing aerobics up to now in PE), indoors because they're doing something with drainage pipes out in the field (we have to use a softer ball because evidently one of the girls almost lost an eye a couple years ago when they were playing inside with the regular field hockey ball).

So out came the little pervo games skirt. On went the tennis shoes and shin guards and gum guards and all that. We had to play in the gym because it was raining outside, and the boys were doing weight training, so of course they had to stop and watch us. It's really not fair, because the guys' PE teacher just tells them what they're to do each day, then he leaves them (Peg says he goes to one of the offtrack-betting places and bets all day), while Miss Ashley, our teacher, stays with us every second of the hour and urges us on.

You know me, Dru: I'm not the most athletic person in the world, although I like tennis and I can do aerobics as long as there's a decent song playing, but the purpose of field hockey escapes me. At least with real hockey you get to ice-skate, but in this sort of hockey, which Holly told me they've played forever, all you do is run around with your shoes squeaking on the gym floor as you chase after a stupid ball. Of course, I got stuck with a bunch of the Snickerers on my team, and despite the fact that Miss Ashley told me to stay in the rear and try to pick up the game as it was played, Snickerer Ann (she's the one with the big wart on her hand) made sure she messed with me every chance she got.

"Hey!" I yelled the first time she whacked me on the shin guards. It hurt!

"Don't be such a crybaby," she sneered.

"Is there a problem, Williams?" Miss Ashley asked.

I glared at Ann and fired up the Emily Cool. "No problem," I said, gritting my teeth (that's all I seem to do around the Snickerers).

Ann and Bee double-teamed me after that (and we were on the same side!), taking turns to smack me on the shins, or "accidentally" hit me with their sticks.

You'll be glad to know that I got in a few good smacks to both of them, but got called out for high-sticking each time.

Right near the end of the game S-Bee waited until Miss Ashley was looking away, then she stuck her stick out as I ran past, which made me fall. S-Ann saw me on the floor and hit the ball to me really hard—straight at my head! I curled up into a fetal ball to keep from being brained by it.

"You had a free shot," S-Ann yelled. "You should have taken it, not laid on the ground and cried like a baby! Don't you know anything?"

"She's American," Snickerer Bee said (her real name is Bertrice, which is awful, but she deserves the name). "Americans are so backward they have to turn around to close the door."

"Oh, I am, like, so offended," I said as I stood up, leaning on my hockey stick and looking mega cool. "Why don't you try making sense next time, Bertrice, it might be a nice change."

"Captain, you didn't call for a time-out," Miss Ashley said, clapping her hands. The guys yelled a few encouraging comments, which Miss Ashley frowned at, but the game resumed. There was a horrible long moment when everything went into slow motion. Miss Ashley was saying something to one of the boys. S-Bee ran over to me and crossed her stick in front of mine so I couldn't move it. S-Ann (who was the forward) tripped another girl to get the ball from her, then took careful aim at me and bashed the ball toward me as hard as she could. The ball didn't skim along the ground, it sailed up into the air, right about chest level. I shoved Bee to the side, and without thinking, swung my stick up like a baseball bat, hitting at the ball really hard. The impact of it hurt my hands, but it was a small price to watch it go flying back toward Ann. Um. Right at her head (you know I was kicked off the girls' softball team because I was a horrible batter).

S-Ann screamed and dropped to the ground to avoid being hit by the ball. The guys laughed. Miss Ashley clapped her hands and yelled for order. S-Bertrice pretended to trip, and slammed into me, knocking me to the ground as well.

Two girls on the other team who were running toward me couldn't stop in time, and tripped over S-Bee, and then they went down as well. Holly dropped her stick in order to help pull S-Bee off me, but she (S-Bee) kicked out at her, so down Holly went. The girl behind her stumbled over Holly's stick, lurching into another girl, who hit the wall and slid down it to the floor.

"Get off me, you perv!" I said as I pushed S-Bee away from me (not an easy job, she weighs as much as a horse) and looked around. Everywhere you looked, there were girls lying on the floor. It was carnage, but a carnage the guys appreciated. I glanced down and realized we were all exposing our undies and stuff. Thank God I kept my nylons on!

"Williams tripped me," S-Bee yelled as soon as she got to her feet. "She put her foot out and deliberately tripped me."

Miss Ashley came over and checked out Mariah, the girl who hit the wall.

"I did not! You almost broke my ribs throwing yourself on me!" I answered, turning to Miss Ashley. "You saw her, didn't you?"

"She did not! I saw it all, Miss Ashley." S-Ann quickly

came to her friend's defense. Weasels do that sort of thing. "Williams did trip Bee, after she tried to hit me in the face with the ball. She high-sticked, too."

"Girls—"

"Honestly, the lies you children spout!" I didn't care if the boys were watching—I was not going to be lied about to my face. Holly hobbled over to stand with me. "Once you're older and have a bit more maturity, you'll understand that you really don't *have* to be a weasel. There is help for weaselitis."

"Weasels!" S-Ann and S-Bee both glared their little beady (weasel) eyes at me.

"If the weasel feet fit, wear 'em!"

The guys hooted.

"Girls, that will be enough!"

"We are not weasels," S-Ann said. "Nor are we a stupid American who thinks she's so much better than us, but is really too dense to do *anything* right."

I waved her words away, hurt by her outrageous claims, but as ever I wasn't going to let them see that. "Obviously, my character is too complex for you to grasp. You'll find out that sort of thing comes with age."

"That will do, Emily. Ann, you and Bee are excused for the rest of the lesson. Please take Mariah with you. Emily, you will report to the headmaster's office."

The Snickerers snickered. The boys groaned their protest that the scene was over. I sighed heavily, and headed toward the locker room to change into my uniform. I know Miss Ashley thought she was punishing me by sending me to see our local Russell Crowe look-alike, but I didn't mind in the least. He always gave me a little lecture about whatever it was I was supposed to have done, but after that he liked to talk about hiking and outdoor stuff. We've spent a lot of time together, and if it weren't for Aidan, I think I could have worked up a pash for him.

I have to go. I'm meeting Holly at the local chemist's (that's a drugstore) to see what sort of stuff they have to coat the handle of my dresser drawer. Don't forget to tell me which job you're picking for work experience. It's too bad you only get to do it for a week—we have a whole month of WE in January. I'm thinking of asking if I can go up to my aunt's in Scotland. She lives on a sheep farm; that ought to qualify as work experience, don't you think?

Later!

Hugs and kisses,
~Em

Subject: I have a life again!
From: Mrs.Oded@btelecom.co.uk
To: Dru@seattlegrrl.com
Date: 26 September 2003 8:43 pm

There's so much to tell you, I don't know where to begin, but first . . .

Dru wrote:
> I bought some condoms for this weekend and hid
> them under my pillow. Ribbed. You don't think that
> was too pushy of me, do you? I mean, won't V have
> some of his own? What if he doesn't? What if he
> wants to do it and I pull out my ribbed condoms and
> he thinks I'm, like, slutty? Should I just mention them

Deep breath, girlfriend. First of all, you are *not* slutty for having condoms. Sheesh, even my mom offered to get me condoms if I wanted them (I didn't, but that's only because Bess gave me some a couple of months ago). That's just smart, and you know it. You don't want to end up like Marvel and have a baby before you graduate. One of my mom's cousins had a girl who got pregnant when she was fourteen. She's almost nineteen now, and she has THREE KIDS!

OK, safe-sex lecture over. Ribbed is very cool, I'm sure. Vance will love them. Just be sure you tell me everything afterward. There's so much no one tells us—if you're going to go first, you have a duty to tell me stuff so I don't make a fool of myself.

My big news is Aidan, Aidan, Aidan, the perfect Mr. Hottie. I saw him heading into the library when I was going to French (calamity *du jour*: toothache. I think Madame Grayson is getting suspicious, though, 'cause she fired a whole lot of French at me and didn't seem too happy when I mumbled into the palm of my hand). Now, you know that I had to be mondo cool with Aidan, since everyone (you and Bess and Holly and Peg and everyone) says he owes me an apology, so I just looked through him and continued on my way to French. He said something, but I couldn't hear what. So I went in to French, and then started worrying. What if the thing that he'd said to me was an apology, and I just walked away from it? He'd think I was being snotty just like the Snickerers said, and then I'd never, ever have him! Obviously I was going to have to go to the library and just hang out and see if he said anything else, or if

◢ 105

he acted cold to me, which meant that he had apologized and I hadn't heard it, and then I'd have to apologize to him for not hearing *his* apology.

I got out of French for a few minutes by having a really loud case of the hiccups that annoyed Miss Grayson until she told me to go drink some water. I ran all the way to the library, then strolled in like I had a free period and was just looking for something. Aidan was sitting with a couple of sixth formers near the front desk. I hung around the career section waiting for him to notice me, which he finally did. He smiled, which was a good sign. It meant that he A) wasn't pissed at me about the night at the club, and B) wasn't pissed that I hadn't heard his apology. If that's what he had said to me.

"There you are. I've been hoping to see you before lunch."

"Oh, Aidan? I didn't see you there," I lied, browsing in the career pamphlets. "I just stopped by for a quick look at info about being a"—I looked down at the pamphlet in my hand—"um, mortician."

He gave a little laugh and tucked a strand of my hair behind my ear. "Mortician?"

"It's a lost art," I said, and waited.

He took the pamphlet from my hands and pulled me over to the career corner where no one ever goes. "I wanted to talk to you, but I was sick with a cold for a few days—"

A cold! Why didn't I think of that? He had a cold! It wasn't me after all! Whew.

"—but I wanted to apologize for Friday. I had a bit too much to drink, you know how it is, out with your mates and things get a bit fuzzy."

Fuzzy? Um. OK.

"But I realize I shouldn't have just left you like I did, and I'm sorry about that. So," he kind of chucked my chin and leaned close until I could smell the mint on his breath, "you forgive me?"

"Sure," I said, wondering if he was going to kiss me right there in the library. I mean, how romantic can you get? I prepared to melt into a big old gooey puddle. "I understand."

"Good girl." He smiled again, and although he didn't kiss me, he did rub his thumb over my bottom lip in a sexy kind of way. I immediately went into panic mode. What did it mean? Dr. Ruth never went into thumb-rubbing! Was I supposed to kiss his thumb? Lick it? Give him a little love bite? Suck on it? WHY DOESN'T ANYONE EVER EXPLAIN THIS STUFF? "Maybe we can go out to the club again."

"That would be über-cool. You know, I'm in charge of the Halloween party this year," I said, waiting for him to ask me to it.

"Are you? Make it a good one then, will you? Usually they're lame."

"Oh, this one is going to be very cool. There's going to be a haunted house for the little kids, and then a dance for the rest of us. Running it is a lot of work, but I think it will be fun." What did I have to do, hit him over the head with a hint?

"Good enough. I have to get back to my mates. We're swotting citizenship."

"Ah. Happy swotting."

He laughed again and shook his head as he left. "You're too much, Emily."

Too much? I started back to French wondering about that. Do you think it's good for me to be too much? Too much as in mondo coolio, or too much as in a stupid American who thinks she's better than everyone else? GAH! I hate this relationship stuff. I'll never understand it. And what do you think he meant by saying maybe we could go out again? It sounded awfully insubstantial to me. Does it sound that way to you? Do you think it sounds like maybe he's getting over his cold and isn't feeling like going out, but as soon as he does, he's going to invite me out? Or do you think it sounds like he has no intentions of ever asking me out again, but is just too nice to tell me because he knows I'll have to go lock myself in my haunted room for the rest of my life? Double gah!

Lunch was OK. With Aidan there, we couldn't talk about him, and he was just as nice and funny as he usually is. He didn't say anything more about going to the club, or about the party, although I mentioned it a couple of times, and even asked Lalla if she was going with her BF Digger. She was. Peg said she was going to go stag, the better to look everyone over. Holly and I talked about it later, and we've decided that it's going to be a costume party. I thought not at first, since it's kind of juvie to dress up in a costume for Halloween, but then Holly had the brilliant idea of making it a Vampire Ball. So we'll have a Goth theme, and everyone is to wear some sort of Goth costume. You have to help me think of something good. Holly says she wants to go as a wraith, but that sounds awfully unsexy.

Gotta run. *Buffy*'s on. Research for the party, you know. Later!

Hugs and kisses,
~Em

Subject: Oh. My. God. OMG!
From: Mrs.Oded@btelecom.co.uk
To: Dru@seattlegrrl.com
Date: 26 September 2003 11:12 pm

Holly just called. Her stepdad works for a paper in Oxford, and he told her that he'd heard that Oded is going to be filming out in Flintlock Forest (about two miles north of here) the week after next! OHMIGOD OHMIGOD OHMIGOD! I have to be there! I have to see him! I have to get my picture with him! Are you green with jealousy? Hahahahahahahah! I'm going to get to meet Oded!

The future Mrs. Fehr,
~Em

Subject: I'm going to kill my sister
From: Mrs.Oded@btelecom.co.uk
To: Dru@seattlegrrl.com
Date: 28 September 2003 1:58 pm

Dru wrote:
> *vampire ball is too cool! You don't need my help,*
> *you're doing fine on your own. I don't know what*
> *you're thinking about a costume, but you definitely*
> *want something that you can can do a his-and-her*
> *thing. Now that Aidan has apologized and is*
> *obviously feeling too remorseful to ask you out,*
> *you'll have to do the thinking for both of you.*

Ooooh, I kind of like the thought of a his-and-her costume. Maybe we could each be a half of a bleeding heart? Or a vampire and his willing victim? OH! I know! What about one of those bondage costumes? I could be Mistress Cruella and he could be my love slave! Yeah, I like that idea!

As you can see by my subject line, I'm going to have to kill Bess. She went too far last night. There's nothing else for it but to kill her. I have never, ever, EVER been so embarrassed, mortified, humiliated, and all those other words as I was last night, and it's all Bess's fault. I formally disowned her as a sister. It was drastic, but I had to do it.

You remember from my e-mail a couple of days ago that Holly and I were going with Bess to some women's thing? A get-in-touch-(HA!)-with-yourself kind of thing? Well, Holly came over last night and we were both wearing leggings and sweaters, because we figured if we had to sit around on the floor and do yoga and meditate and stuff, we might as well be comfortable, and besides, there were not going to be any boys there. So it didn't matter what we looked like. Bess drove Dad's car (stupid law says I can't drive until I'm seventeen even though I have a license) to Alling, a nearby town that is still lacking because it has no mall, but at least it has a movie theater and swimming pool.

We went into Bess's kind-of-BF's sister's house (the Monk guy with the scraggly hair), and everyone was sitting in the living room having healthy snackies and drinking juice and stuff like that. Chanting music played in the background. Lots of big pillows were scattered on the floor. I figured it would be a couple of hours of "inner goddess" time, and then we'd be off for home so I could figure out a way to get Aidan to invite me to the party.

Holly and I sat down on some pillows near a corner, and all of a sudden, rather than the lights dimming, a bunch more were turned on, and Monk's sister came out with a big box. She started handing stuff out, but while she was doing that, the women around us began taking off their clothes. Holly made kind of a choking sound. I thought her eyes were going to pop out of her head.

"Oh, my God," I said, looking at all the women around us as clothes went flying. "My sister is a lesbian and she's dragged us into an orgy! Oh, my God. OHMIGOD! Quick, Holly, run for the door. I'll distract them until you get out. Call my mom if I don't come out right after you!"

Holly jumped up and stood like a deer in headlights. I scrambled to my feet and prepared to follow Holly, but Bess came over waving a couple of clear plastic things that looked like deranged nutcrackers with long bills at us. "What's the matter with you two? You look like you've seen a ghost."

"Ghosts I can deal with, but this little orgy you've planned will have to go ahead without us. We're not into that sort of thing, and you can just *bet* I'm going to be telling Mom what sort of stuff you are doing behind her back."

Bess rolled her eyes and shoved a plastic thing at each of us. "It's not an orgy, stupid, it's a self-awareness party. I told you that."

I looked around. Everyone was laughing and chatting and acting just like they weren't all naked. "You are too strange, Bess. I don't need to get naked to be self-aware. You can have your plastic thing back. I won't need it."

"Problems?" Monk's sister came up, the only one

besides Bess and Holly and me who still had her clothes on. Holly was staring over my shoulder in horror at a woman who was on a floor pillow. She had the plastic thingy and was shoving the bill part up her woo! HER WOO!

"Don't look," I whispered to Holly, and had to forcibly turn her around so she wouldn't see the orgy. "I'll get you for this, Bess, so help me God, I will! Holly is sensitive! You're shocking her!"

"Stop being such a little twit," she said, then turned to the M's S. "No problem; they just don't understand what the purpose of the evening is."

The M's sister laughed. "No wonder you have those surprised looks on your faces. You're holding a speculum, a tool used by gynecologists to examine your vagina and cervix."

I turned about a hundred shades of red. Holly weaved where she stood, like she was going to pass out or something. I grabbed her arm and held her upright.

"The purpose of this evening is to examine our cervixes, and become familiar and comfortable with our femininity and reproductive organs."

OHMIGOD!

"Why?" I asked, horrified (can you *imagine?*). "Why do you want to look at it?"

The M's S smiled and patted me on the arm. "The pelvis is an area of a woman's anatomy that is often a mystery to us. Self exams offer us the ability to really know our bodies, even that part that we don't normally see. As your knowledge of yourself and your body grows, you will take back the power to care for yourself, to know what your body is going through, and to understand the changes that happen over time."

Holly sank down onto the floor into a blob-like shape, whimpering quietly to herself.

"If I wanted to see cervixes, I'd be a doctor," I told the Monk's sister. "What you're talking about is just gross!"

"It's fascinating, Em, it really is. You can see everything. It's pretty amazing down there. Did you know that the walls of your vagina are a pretty, glistening pink?"

"BESS!" I yelled, clutching my hands in front of my crotch, which was silly, because my sweater reached down my thighs. She couldn't possibly see into my woo.

"Don't be such an idiot, Em. You have to take back your own body!"

I grabbed Holly and pulled her up to her feet. Her eyes looked wild, like she wasn't aware of her surroundings. I pushed her toward the door. I had no idea how we were going to get home, but I didn't care. I just wanted out of that den of cervix-peekers.

"The medical industry has hijacked our bodies," the Monk's sister said, following with Bess as Holly and I staggered to the door. "They've stripped us of our autonomy. We have to take back what's our due."

"Ignorance is enslavement," Bess added. "Don't rely on someone else for knowledge about your body, learn to love yourself. Empower yourself. Examine yourself. Touch yourself!"

"EEEEEK!" I shrieked as I saw what the woman with the plastic speculum was doing. She had a flashlight and a mirror and was LOOKING UP HER WOO! I could see it! "I'd rather die! Go away! Leave us alone! We don't want empowerment, we just want to be ignorant! Ignorance is bliss! STOP TOUCHING ME WITH THAT THING!"

Holly made a gabbling sound, and I was sure she was going to ralph, so I flung the door open and shoved her through it.

"Emily, come back here!"

"I'm going to tell Mom!" I yelled at Bess, then turned and ran after Holly as she raced down the path to the street.

It was raining (that's all it does in this country), but honest to Pete, Dru, neither Holly nor I noticed it. We wandered around a bit, holding each other up and kind of half-crying and gasping and stuff. Holly was shaking so hard her teeth chattered, but at last we pulled ourselves together and found a bus that would take us back to POTW. We made it home and raced up the stairs. Mom called something up to me, but I didn't stay around to hear what it was. We got to my room (for once my underwear wasn't scattered everywhere), and I locked the door, then Holly and I dragged the dresser over to the door in case Bess tried to break it down to force us to examine our cervixes.

Dru, I have never in my life been so embarrassed! I could have died! Not only at that stupid speculum party, but then I had to explain to Holly that I wasn't really related to Bess, that Mom and Brother adopted her (they didn't, but Holly doesn't know that) and thus her actions are not contagious. Holly was so upset she had to have her brother come and pick her up because she was too shaky to walk home.

I filled Mom in about what happened, and she told me that those sorts of things went on, and if I didn't want to participate, I didn't have to, and no, it didn't mean that Bess was a lesbian or certifiably insane. She also denied my request to formally disown Bess and throw her out, which I think pretty much shows you that Bess is the family favorite. I bet if I ran around shoving speculums up myself and showing everyone my cervix they'd kick me out pretty darn fast!

Anyway, Bess came down the next morning and started to read me a lecture about how I embarrassed her in front of her friends, but I told her I was de-sistering her, and therefore she was a stranger, and since I didn't know her, I didn't have to listen to her. So I didn't.

The only bad thing about this is that Holly and I were counting on Bess to take us Oded hunting next week. Now we'll have to find another way to get to Flintlock Forest. Poop.

I can't wait to hear about your weekend. E-mail me as soon as Vance leaves, and don't leave out ANYTHING!

Hugs and kisses,
~Em

Subject: Well, I tried. Again.
From: Mrs.Oded@btelecom.co.uk
To: Dru@seattlegrrl.com
Date: 28 September 2003 8:33 pm

Why haven't you e-mailed me yet? What are you doing? Well, no I guess you don't have to tell me exactly what you're doing . . . no, wait, yes, you do! I need to know what it feels like and what you did, and what he did, and whether you laughed, and where you put your hands, and all that stuff. Sheesh. I can't believe you haven't e-mailed me. Even with the time difference, it's still after noon. I mean, even if you are gettin' it on with V, you have to take a break sometime! Don't you?

Well, while you're shacked up with your love bunny (or in V's case, love weasel), let me tell you what happened this afternoon. Holly and I went shopping on High Street to try to find some sort of dye that I could use on the undie-drawer handle (undies are currently residing in my pants drawer. I guess only the top drawer is haunted, because so far no undies have appeared without my permission), and we ran into Devon and Fang. No Aidan—he said he had to stay home this weekend and make up all the work he missed at school while he was out with a cold (and there's something going on about that—I'll tell you in a mo), but still, it was nice to meet Devon and Fang. We went to a café on Second Street and drank coffee and looked really sophisticated and stuff with D&F—one on either side of each of us, how cool is that?—and then Devon told us he's having a party at his house in a fortnight (that's two weeks—why can't these people just SAY things properly?).

"You both should come. It's going to be a stunner."

I looked at Holly. She looked kind of worried (her best look), but I knew that I had to be at this stunner party or I'd die. "I'd love to go, thanks, Devon. Holly would love to go, too."

"Maybe. It depends on my mum."

Devon smiled at her, then transferred his smile to me, and I have to tell you, Dru, I started to reevaluate my deep, boundless love for Aidan. I don't mean that I'd leave Aidan for Devon, but he is awfully cute, and he is eighteen, and he can be drop-dead sexy when he wants to be.

"Aidan's going to be there, isn't he?"

"Of course." Devon laughed. "It wouldn't be a party without our best mixer."

I tried to look sophisticated and nonchalant and all that, but I know now what a mixer is (it's a guy who "mixes it up" with girls). Oh, yeah, that's just what I want to hear about the man who is probably my once and future husband.

"I'm surprised he's not here by now," Devon said, looking at his watch. "We always meet here on Sundays."

Note to self: Be in the surrounding area every Sunday afternoon.

"He's probably still fagged out from going to London," Fang said.

"London?" I asked. Aidan went to London?

"I told you he's our best mixer." Devon took my hand and started rubbing my fingers. Devon is one of those touchy-feely guys, something I don't normally mind because it looks very cool to have someone holding your hand or rubbing your arm, but there's a time and a place for finger rubbing, and this wasn't it. "Aid went up to town with Quint and a couple of birds."

Quint is Aidan's older brother.

"Oh," I said, trying not to look like the world had just ended, which, of course, it had. My life is hell once again. "Um. When did he do that?"

"Earlier in the week. We did warn you he's a mixer." Devon gave me a pitying look, which was almost, but not quite, as bad as Pity Kisses. "Not like me, now. I know how to treat a bird properly."

Fang snorted and almost shot beer through his nose again. "Pull the other one, mate."

I just sat there feeling miserable while they ribbed each other, and Holly sent me little worried glances. Now, I'm not saying that Aidan outright lied to me, but how could he have missed time in school because he was out with a cold, and be in London at the same time? With girls. Maybe he went on Wednesday or Thursday, after he was feeling better, but not well enough to go to school. Yeah, that makes sense. He wouldn't lie to me, but he might have just forgotten to tell me about going to London. Whew! Glad I got that figured out, and no, don't tell me it doesn't make sense, because you'll just have to trust me that it does, OK? OK.

Devon and Fang walked us to the bus, which was pretty cool because the people waiting got to see us with them. Fang didn't say much, true to form, but he did smile at me a couple of times and held my coat for me when we were leaving the café, which made up a lot for the Pity Kiss. Even though I know Bess was wrong about him having a thing for me, I decided that he deserved to be rewarded for being thoughtful, so I pushed him into the number three slot of Perfect Men For Emily list (behind Devon, who was really good at flirting). Just in case, you understand. I mean, it's not like I'm really interested in him or anything.

Devon gave me a kiss on the cheek, which was *very* cool. He didn't give one to Holly, though, which made me feel bad for her. Just because she's a year younger doesn't mean she doesn't want to be kissed on the cheek, too. I made a mental note to ask Fang if he'd be extra-special nice to her at the party, since I figure they are both kind of shy and quiet. They might hit it off.

Then again, they probably won't. I mean, Fang deserves someone a little more lively, if you know what I mean (and that's no slur on Holly. You'd like her, she's really sweet, if a bit on the timid side). No, come to think of it, Holly isn't at all Fang's type, but still, it can't hurt to ask him to be nice to her.

This week is going to be interesting at school. The new Web page that Holly and Astrid and I did, and über-cool chat room which no other school in this area has, is about to go live. Astrid is a foreign exchange student from Denmark. She's OK, except she smells weird. I think it's all the cheese she eats.

In addition to that, we're going to have more hockey, which means I'm going to have to take SA and SB down a peg or two, or put up with their stupid attempts to get me into trouble (I think they're working with the Duff, frankly). But most importantly, Holly and I will be on Oded Watch.

We were worried about how we'd get there until Holly suggested riding our bikes. Actually she said we could cycle there, which made me think she had a motorcycle until I realized how much sense that made. Not only is the driving age here sixteen, Holly is just *not* a biker chick.

"Cycle as in bicycle?" I asked, figuring it was better to make sure. You never knew with shy people. Sometimes they can surprise you. Fang did, even if all he surprised me with was a Pity Kiss.

"Yes. It should only take us a half hour to ride there, and we can chain the cycles together to a tree."

"Sounds like a good plan, except for one thing," I said, putting a little bit of Ooh La La blush on her (I was trying to show her how the right makeup can accentuate rather than just lie on her skin like a layer of Marmite). "I don't have a bike. Cycle. Either."

"Oh, Peter does." Peter is her older brother. He's twenty-three, and engaged to a girl who lives in Holland who is six years older than him. "He won't mind if you use it. He never rides it anymore."

"Cool. Then that's what we'll do."

"But, Emily," she said, turning around as I was dusting her with bronzer, which totally *ruined* the cheekbone highlighting I had just done, and you know how hard it is to get cheekbones on someone who doesn't have them! "We'll only be able to go after three, and I'll have to be home by five or Mum will want to know where I've been, so with the travel time, that only leaves us an hour to find Oded. Do you think we can do it?"

"Who says we're going to leave at three?" I smiled a smug little smile and accented her eyebrows (newly plucked—I refuse to see my friends growing Unibrows) with a Roasted Chestnut eyebrow pencil. "You're a key member of the Vampire Ball planning committee, aren't you?"

"Yes," she said slowly, watching me carefully.

"And I'm the head of the very same planning committee."

She thought for a minute. "Yes."

"And I am allowed to call meetings of the planning committee if they have free time, right?"

"Right."

I waited for it to sink in. Evidently she needed a little help. "So I'll just call a meeting between you and me, and we'll talk about party stuff on our way to see Oded! Brilliant, isn't it?"

Her eyes got really big, and she squeaked a bit when she talked. "But that would mean leaving the school grounds."

"Yeah, so?" I pulled out the Moonlit Rose blush and gave myself just a little touch-up dab.

"That's against the rules."

I smiled at her in the mirror. "Rules are for sheep, Holly. You and I aren't sheep—we're stunningly sexy women who are too cool to be tied down to mundane little rules meant for people like Ann and Bertrice."

"But—"

"No one will know. Now stop being such a wimp and repeat after me: Oded is hunkalicious."

"Oded is hunkalicious," she said, looking miserable.

"Oded is droolworthy."

"Droolworthy?"

"Droolworthy."

"Oded is droolworthy."

"Oded is mine. Well, Oded is Emily's, but she's going to share him with me."

She repeated it, but she didn't look like she believed it. She'll soon learn that nothing stands in the way of me and my once and future husband. Oh, wait, I said that about Aidan, didn't I? Well, maybe I'll be married twice. Or just once if a certain hottie went to London on Monday, rather than being sick . . . no, I'm sure he didn't, I'm sure it was later, after he was feeling better. I'm just being suspicious.

I can't believe it's after one your time and you STILL haven't e-mailed me! Criminy, girl! Think about someone else for a change, would you?

Hugs and kisses,
~Em

Subject: Re: What should I do?
From: Mrs.Oded@btelecom.co.uk
To: Dru@seattlegrrl.com
Date: 29 September 2003 7:02 pm

Dru wrote:
> *We played games and watched movies together,*
> *and he kissed me a lot, which was also really nice.*
> *And he, you know, touched me and things, but he*
> *didn't get . . . you know . . . that way. I'm a little*
> worried, Em. You don't think it's me that's making
> him floppy, do you?

Well. I have to say, I'm a bit relieved that it didn't happen. I know you wanted it and all, and I know you think
that the V is Mr. Perfect (although how you can over-
look him going out with Tabitha and not telling you
about it is beyond me), but honestly, Dru, you're too
good for him. But I'm your friend, so I'll stand by you no
matter what you do. Did you read *How to Make Love
All Night*? Heidi said it's full of stuff that men do. I
haven't read it yet (I doubt if they have it over here), but
she said it made a lot of difference between her and
Thom. Maybe you should get a copy for Vance? Or
what about that Viagra stuff? I used to get a lot of
spams for that, it sounds pretty good and maybe that
would help. I'll ask Mom about it for you.

I'm glad you had a good weekend regardless. I know
you're miffed about missing swimming, but I'm sure it
won't take you too long to catch back up to the rest of
the team once you get the cast off. Just don't let Miss
Donwell give your spot to Connie.

Gotta run. I have a ton of homework to do still, and
we're going live with the chat room this week, so I
have to make sure the stupid server is set up right.
Holly and I are going Oded hunting on Wednesday.
You're jealous, aren't you? Sure you are. Wish us luck!

I'll send you piccies.

Hugs and kisses,
~Em

Subject: Viagra is totally green
From: Mrs.Oded@btelecom.co.uk
To: Dru@seattlegrrl.com
Date: 29 September 2003 9:46 pm

Mom says it works, so if Vance can get some, I think it would probably help. If I get another Viagra spam, I'll forward it to you so you can send it to him.

Chat server is totally flaky. I'm going to have to have Mr. Thorpe beat it into submission. I hate JavaScript!

Later, chicky!

Hs and Ks,
~Em

Subject: Oded, Day One
From: Mrs.Oded@btelecom.co.uk
To: Dru@seattlegrrl.com
Date: 1 October 2003 6:37 pm

I just noticed this ISP makes the dates English (backward). Huh. Weird.

Well, Day One of Oded Hunt was pretty much a scratch. We rode out to the FF despite the fact that it was raining and we got totally soaked. Once we got there, I suddenly realized the mistake I'd made—I was still in the dead-grotty school uniform! OMG! Oded would see me in that, and think I was a little kid! So all in all, I'm glad we didn't see him, although we did see his trailer, which was mondo über coolio.

There's some sort of castle in the middle of the forest, which is what the film company is there for. We skipped out of the last two classes and our study period, and made it there by 1:30. We found a spot to hide the bikes (Holly forgot to bring a lock, something else we'll remember for tomorrow), and then ran around the edges until we spotted some cars. Then we strolled up all casual-like, and got to see some of the movie people. Mostly they were the cameramen and stuff, but there were two women in medieval costume, and a guy dressed like a knight who was practicing sword fighting with another guy who wasn't dressed like a knight. No one paid us any attention, so we wandered around a bit, then Holly saw a clump of trailers. Oded's had his name on it, but it was dark, so evidently he wasn't there. I wanted to ask someone when he'd be back, but Holly was too afraid that they'd throw us out, so I just hid behind a Porta Potti and eavesdropped on a couple of guys talking about the shooting schedule. They didn't mention Oded, but they said the fight scene was going to be shot tomorrow, assuming the weather is better. We'll go out again tomorrow. I am not letting this fabulous chance slip through my fingers!

Oh, I have to share this, it's such a hoot! I told you about the new Web site going live, right? I divvied up the work so Holly and Astrid got the easy stuff, and kept the harder stuff for myself, like setting up the chat room and the important parts that the teachers are going to look at (I'm no fool!).

Astrid and I were doing one final check of links and stuff before I uploaded the final version of the Web site when suddenly she started laughing.

"Whazzup?" I asked, wondering if I didn't spell check something, or if there was yet another embarrassing word mix-up like what happened to me a couple of weeks ago when I confused the words "chuffed" (which means thrilled), and "chuffing" (which means farting).

"You can't put this up!" she said, still laughing, pointing at the screen. "You'll get into so much trouble."

I peeked. "Poop. I linked to the wrong version."

It was the staff bios, of course, the ones I told you that Holly and I did late one night last week when we were watching *Buffy* and eating some really delish Death by Chocolate ice cream, and we got a little silly (you know how massive amounts of chocolate can do that to you). Anyway, I thought I'd linked to the proper (boring) bios, but I guess not.

"Don't worry. I'll take care of that just as soon as I get the GSCE board up."

Astrid didn't say anything more, and I was busy trying to get the stupid software the school bought for the message boards to format properly, and by the time I was done, I had to go to lunch, and then Holly and I left to go hunt Oded, and . . . well, I forgot to make the change. Luckily I remembered in time, and changed the bios to the proper page, but I thought you'd like to see a bit of what Holly and I can do under the influence of *Buffy* and extreme chocolate.

Martine Ashley
  Physical Education
  Edinburgh University, Scotland
  Postgraduate Certificate in Education

Teaching 2 Years

"I believe the key to a good education is found by playing hockey. Not only will the pervy skirts teach you what it's like to be ogled by boys who don't have anything better to do than to try to peek at your knickers; you will understand better the nature of sport and sportsmanship, and learn that the only way to succeed is to stomp all over your teammates."

Elizabeth Spreadborough
    English
    Bachelor of Science in Education (a gazillion years ago)
    Bachelor of Arts in English
    Massey University, New Zealand
    Teaching 17 Years
    Deaf as a Doornail

"WHAT? WHAT'S THAT YOU SAY? SPEAK UP, WILL YOU? OH, WHAT DOES TEACHING MEAN TO ME? ORGANIZATION! ORGANIZATION IS THE KEY! WITHOUT ORGANIZATION, YOU HAVE NOTHING, NOTHING AT ALL! AND NO PDAS! HATE THE LITTLE BUGGERS."

Emmeline "Horseface" Naylor
    Physics/Head of Year 11
    Bristol University
    Master in Physics
    Teaching 24 Years

"Students should be humiliated at every opportunity so they don't discover that they're smarter than we are. And they shouldn't be allowed to talk back. Or neigh in the hallways when I walk by. What's with that? Stupid students."

Damien Krigon
   Headmaster
   General Studies/Latin
   University of Cambridge
   Master in Latin
   Lancaster University
   Postgraduate Certificate in Education
   Teaching 20 Years

   "Students like me because I look like Russell Crowe will in about ten years. In other words, I'm totally snack-worthy. Worship me."

   So what's going on with you and the Man? Are you going to see him again this weekend? Did your mom find out that Heidi didn't come over last weekend? I'm dying for some news.

   Hugs and kisses,
   ~Em

Subject: re: It's raining here, too
From: Mrs.Oded@btelecom.co.uk
To: Dru@seattlegrrl.com
Date: 2 October 2003 8:17 pm

Dru wrote:
> *I told Vance about Viagra. BIG MISTAKE. He got all*
> *huffy with me and said, "What, you think I'm*
> *impotent now?" and it took me forever to get him*
> *back in a happy mood. So thanks, but I think I'll*
> *have to pass on the Viagra, unless you can think of*
> *a way for me to give it to him without him knowing.*

Hmm. Well, you could bake it into brownies or something. Or maybe grind it up and put it in something thick, like soup or a milkshake or something. Or tell him it's a love vitamin (which it kind of is, if you think about it) and that you're only giving it to him because you don't want him to get low on electrolytes and stuff. Oh, how do I know? It's not really important, is it? It's not like you guys are doing it.

Day Two of Odeding was pretty much the same as Day One, except we were late getting out because of the IT stuff, and then Holly didn't want to go, and I spent twenty minutes convincing her that no one would notice that we were skipping school. Then I forgot my change of clothes, and I had to go back and get that, so when we got to Oded Ground Central, there was no one there. I think it was because it was still raining. There were only a couple of guys around, so we left and went back to school, since Holly was making such a fuss. The weather guy said tomorrow should be clear, so we're going to go back. If I don't get to see Oded because of the stupid weather, I'm never going to forgive Brother for dragging me here in the first place! It's just downright cruel to taunt me with Oded and not let me see him!

Oh, hang on, Brother wants to talk to me about something. BRB.

Hugs and kisses,
~Em

Subject: Why can't I have NORMAL parents?
From: Mrs.Oded@btelecom.co.uk

OH. MY. GOD. You are not going to believe what just happened. Brother came in while I was e-mailing you and said he wanted to talk to me. So, being the good little daughter who suffers *everything* just to keep her parents happy, I logged off and toddled into the small room Brother calls his study (he's getting *so* lord of the manor). Mom was there, too, which should have been a big red-light warning, but all I could think was that someone ratted on me going Oded hunting.

"Sit down, Emily. Your mother and I thought it was time to have a talk with you. Er . . . another talk with you."

Crap. Someone *had* told them. I started thinking up all sorts of reasons why Oded was much more important to my health and happiness than going to school all day, every day.

Brother sat opposite me, on a leather couch next to Mom, who was smiling in that bright, chippy, "I've got some bad news for you" sort of way. "Your mother told me that you were inquiring a few days ago about . . . er . . . a substance used to give men stamina."

Huh? I blinked at him and wondered if he was hallucinating, or if he'd finally just gone dotty.

"Sexual stamina," Mom said.

I moved my blink to her. Why on earth would I be asking her about sexual stamina?

"Viagra," Brother added.

"Oh, that. Yeah. What about it?"

Brother jumped up and started pacing around the room, clearing his throat and tugging at his shirtsleeves.

"You asking about the Viagra brought to our attention that you're sixteen now, and might be interested in . . . er . . . experimenting."

"Not really," I said, wondering what bee got up his butt. Boy, you ask someone about a little Viagra, and they go all psycho on you. "I'm taking chemistry only because it looks good on the transcripts, and besides, the only other science class they had was biology, and that totally sucks."

Brother stopped and stared at me. "Emily, what are you talking about?"

I rolled my eyes. Honestly, was the man losing his hearing, too? "Chemistry."

His Unibrow got all scrunched together as he stood at the end of the couch and frowned at me. Mom started snickering.

"Why?" he asked.

"Why what?"

"Why are you telling me about chemistry when I'm trying to talk to you about . . . er . . . experimenting?"

"Do you have a whiteboard? I can write it out in big letters for you—I don't like chemistry!"

"Dear, she doesn't understand—" Mom started to say, but Brother interrupted her.

"Well that much is obvious, Chris. How can a girl have such a high GPA but be so clueless about real life?"

"Clueless!" I gasped. Me? Clueless? Was he *mad?*

Mom smiled and patted him on the arm. "Sometimes the smartest girls are the ones who are the most naïve."

"I am so not naïve! I am the least naïve person I know!"

Brother did a little nostril flare which you really don't want me to describe. "Now, listen to me, Emily. I'm trying to be sympathetic and understanding and all that rot, despite the fact that when I was your age my mother would have sewn my pants shut before she let me go near a girl, but still, your mother says we have to give you some space and respect, so I'm trying to give it to you. All right?"

"Maybe," I said carefully, confused as heck. "What does Grandma have to do with chemistry?"

"God above, she's trying to drive me mad!" Brother yelled, running his hands through his hair and instantly forming the hair horn.

Mom laughed.

"This is your doing, isn't it?" he asked, rounding on her. "This is all part of that women's lib stuff you've taught them, isn't it? One daughter is out gallivanting around the country, protesting everything that takes her fancy and talking about shacking up with a noncelibate monk, and the other is calmly inquiring about Viagra!"

Now, that was interesting. I had no idea Bess was thinking about moving in with Monk.

"Brother, calm down," Mom said, still laughing. "If you'll just tell her what you're talking about—"

"Do you want to do this?" he asked, kind of snapping the words at her, his hands on his hips.

She shook her head and laughed even harder. "You wanted another child. We made a deal—I'd talk to Bess; you talk to Emily."

"I didn't know I was going to get the Viagra daughter! The deal's off."

"Hello," I said, waving my hand. "Is anyone aware of the fact that the Viagra daughter is sitting right here in the room? Isn't it bad for my psyche for you to be talking about me like that? You don't want to scar me for life. I'll need therapy."

Brother took a deep breath and let it out slowly. "Emily."

I tipped my head on the side and looked at him. I suppose in a father kind of way he looked cute, all hair-horned and Unibrowed, and with a twitch that had appeared out of nowhere. "Yo!"

"You are sixteen."

"Yup. Have been since April."

"You have asked about Viagra."

Weasels feasting on my tender flesh would never pry from my lips the fact that I was asking about Viagra because your BF is also known as Mr. Floppy. "You're two for two—would you like to risk it all for the grand-prize round?"

He closed his eyes for a minute, then opened them up again. They were bloodshot. "Your mother assures me that you have learned the pertinent facts from both her and the school."

A horrible suspicion started to grow in the back of my mind. He couldn't be talking about . . . Oh, God, he couldn't, could he? The very last thing I ever expected him to talk to me about?

"You are a young woman, a young woman with a lively and naturally curious mind, one who enjoys new experiences."

Maybe I was wrong. Maybe I was imagining it. "Yeah, but not chemistry—"

"SEX!" he bellowed suddenly, making my eyes almost pop out with surprise. "Dammit, I'm talking about sex, girl! Sexual intercourse! Between you and a boy . . . er . . . " He looked at Mom. "It is boys she's interested in?"

Mom nodded.

"That's good. Although if it was the other, at least we wouldn't have to worry about her getting pregnant—"

"AAAAAAAaaaaaaaaaaaaaaargh!" I screamed, unable to stand hearing them talk about me like that. SEX! Brother was talking to me about sex! "Stop it! I don't want to hear this! I had the sex talk with Mom years ago! Isn't it illegal or something for you to be talking to me about it now? Oh, God, I'm going to *die!*"

"Emily, behave yourself. You're upsetting Brother."

"I'm upsetting *him?*" I stared at Mom, my mouth hanging open, which just goes to show you how upset *I* was, because I never hang my mouth open. It's just so uncool. "What about me?"

Mom sighed, pulled Brother down to the couch, then leaned forward. "We're concerned that you might be ready to take the step forward to sexual intimacy, and we want you to know that as long as you use protection, we will support your decision. It would make us much happier if you decided to wait, but I realize there are immense pressures on young people these days, and I just want you to be safe. You remember those condoms I mentioned a few months ago?"

"Condoms?" Brother asked, all suspicious-like.

I nodded.

"I want you to have them now. Better safe than sorry," she said.

"What condoms? You offered the girl condoms?"

"Bess gave me some," I said, too embarrassed to say anything else.

"You gave our daughter condoms before I could have the sex talk with her?"

"We want you to be happy, Emily, but most important of all is that you don't do anything that you'll regret

133

later, so we're asking you to promise us that if you do decide to have sex with Aidan or any of the other boys you've met here, you'll use a condom."

"Two condoms," Brother said, still running his hands through his hair. "One can break; use two. Maybe three would be better. That's not too much to ask, is it?"

I stared at my shoes and nodded. On top of everything I started to get all puddly. I mean, it was embarrassing as hell, but kind of nice in a weird sort of way. At least they cared about me. Lalla's mom didn't care what she did at all.

Mom reached over and patted my knee. "You know you can ask us anything, or Bess if you don't want to talk to Brother or me."

I nodded again, and sniffled back more tears. I had to get out of there before they wanted to hug me or something like that.

"It's not like you can shock us. I know you think we're older than the hills, but your father and I have a very healthy sexual relationship, so don't be afraid to ask us about things that might seem strange to you."

"TMI, Mom!" I said, giving her a look.

"TMI?"

"Too much information! I don't want to know about you guys having sex! It's just too icky!"

"Emily, it's a natural part of life—"

"TMI! TMI!" I jumped up and ran for the door. If she was going to start talking about the sort of things her and Brother did, I had to get out of there. Major ew!

"You gave her condoms?" Brother asked as I ran out the door. "Just like that? You didn't talk to me at all, you just offered the girl condoms?"

IT WAS AWFUL! At least when Mom had the Talk with

me, I knew it was coming because the school was doing Sex Ed that quarter. And Brother wasn't there. I mean, it's just too embarrassing. And then for Mom to start telling me about them . . . parent sex! GAH!

I'm so wigged out, I can't even remember what I was going to tell you, so I'm going to bed and try to erase the words "your father and I have a very healthy sexual relationship" from my mind.

You're *so* lucky your dad lives in Dallas.

Hugs and kisses,
~Em

Subject: It figures
From: Mrs.Oded@btelecom.co.uk
To: Dru@seattlegrrl.com
Date: 2 October 2003 9:14 pm

SimEmily died.

Gah.
~Em

Subject: re: Heidi is SUCH a b*tch!
From: Mrs.Oded@btelecom.co.uk
To: Dru@seattlegrrl.com
Date: 5 October 2003 4:01 pm

Dru wrote:
> *said I was obsessing about him, but I'm not, am I?*
> *Do you think I'm obsessing? Obsessing means you*

> can't talk about anything else, and I talk about other
> stuff all the time. I don't bore you with Vance, and
> how wonderful and perfect and fabu-coolio he is,
> do I? So I told Heidi she was just jealous and maybe
> she'd better start thinking about getting a BOB
> instead of waiting for a real one.

OHMIGOD, you didn't tell her to get a battery-operated boyfriend! You didn't! Hoooooot! That is too killer, Dru, it really is. What did she say? And no, you're not obsessed, you're just in love, which is almost as bad, but not quite. I mean, there is other stuff in life than a guy! There's . . . um . . . well, school, only that's not quite the same, but there is other stuff, I just can't think of it right now. Still, that was totally out of line for Heidi to say that. She's obviously never been in love, although she always says she is. Don't worry about her—she's not your real friend. I am, and you can obsess to me about Weasel Boy all you want.

Well, the Official Oded Watch has come to a close. I'm so frustrated, I could just scream. Holly and I went out there every friggin' day, and either they weren't shooting because of the stupid rain, or we just missed him, or we were too early. Today was the last straw. Holly's mom drove us out there, and I thought we might be in luck because there were a ton of people running around doing stuff. There were some actors I didn't recognize in costume standing around talking quietly, and the sword guy showing someone else how to throw a knife, and some guy with a megaphone yelling that it would just be a few more minutes and then they'd do a take. Well, we waited for TWO WHOLE HOURS and no Oded.

Finally I got tired of standing around in the cold in my über-cool black velvet coat and grabbed a guy with a clipboard who was running around handing out cups of coffee. "Excuse me, can you tell me when the shooting is scheduled to begin?"

Didn't that sound cool? Notice I didn't come right out and ask where Oded was. You have to be very tight in these sorts of situations. Stars like Oded get all sorts of weirdo fans who stalk him everywhere. I didn't want this guy thinking I was like that.

He frowned at his hand (some of the coffee had sloshed over onto his fingers). "Just as soon as Mac is happy with the lighting."

"Mac?" I asked.

"The director." He looked up and his eyes got all squinty as he looked me over. "Who are you?"

"Me? Oh, I'm . . . um . . . well, she's connected with the *Oxford Gazette*," I said, pointing at Holly. It's true, her stepdad works for that paper, so she's kind of connected to it by marriage. Holly made a gasping noise, but I ignored her, because suddenly I had the most brilliant idea! I held up my digital camera. "I'm her photographer. She's here to do an interview with Mr. Oded Fehr."

"Oh. Well, you're too late. Oded finished shooting this morning. He's gone back to the studio to do the interior shots."

DAMN!

"Will he be back tomorrow?" I asked, really professional-like.

He shook his head. "We're done filming here just as soon as we get this last shot."

DOUBLE DAMN!

CRAP WITH EXTRA HELPINGS ON TOP!
WAAAAAAAAAAAH!

I'm so bummed. Oded, within a half hour of me, dressed like a knight, and I missed him! I swear to you, Dru, sometimes I think someone has cursed me or put a hex on me or something, because I can't think of one other person who has as crappy luck as I have.

I'm going to work on Mom to see if she'll take us over to Kenworth Studios (where Oded is filming). She's been really nice and all "I'm your friend as well as your mother" ever since the AWFUL SEX TALK, so she should be glad of a chance to do this for me. I'm printing up a couple of ID cards that say that Holly and I are with the newspaper, and I'm going to laminate them. Maybe that will get us in to "interview" Oded.

I have to go. I kind of killed SimOded, and I want to make a new one, and another SimEmily. Oh, hey, I'm thinking of dyeing my hair. Bess had henna put on hers, which makes it a really cool goldy-red. I know it wouldn't be the same on mine, since I have awful dish-water-blond hair (thanks, Mom), but I think it's time for a change. Mom said no when I asked her about henna, but she didn't say no, I couldn't dye my hair, so I think I'll take the last of my birthday money and go down to the hair place next to where Tash works (the only one in town that isn't full of purple-haired old ladies), and get it done. Do you think I should go lighter blond, a real blond, or should I go for dramatic? I kind of fancy myself with raven blue-black hair. Let me know what you think. I want to get it done before the Vampire Ball.

Aidan still hasn't asked me. I've got to do something or else I won't have a date for the über-coolio party that I organized!

I hate life.

Hugs and kisses,
~Em

Subject: Details of the ghost or entity at
249 Basque Close
From: Ewilliams7@gobottle.co.uk
To: enquiries@prs.org
Cc: Mrs.Oded@btelecom.co.uk
Cc: Dru@seattlegrrl.com
Date: 8 October 2003 11:19 am

Dear Psychic Research Society,
  I am an American living in a house at 249 Basque
Close, Piddlington-on-the-Weld, Oxfordshire, and my
underwear drawer is haunted by some sort of ghost or
entity or poltergeist or whatever else would be likely to
haunt an underwear drawer and routinely throw underwear around the room when I'm not around.
  At first I thought it was my parents having a bit of fun,
but after extensive tests (see below), it has become crys-
tal clear that nothing human could be getting in and
rummaging around my undies. It's getting a bit old having to pick up everything almost every single day. I heard
on the television (aka "telly") about your ghost-hunting
teams that go around England trying to get proof of
ghosts, and thought you might want to send them out
to investigate my underwear drawer. I'm sure my parents wouldn't mind, and frankly, I'm willing to bet
there's more than one ghost in this house. It's really old
and it makes a lot of noise at night. The basement is
probably crawling with ghosts.

Thank you.

Emily Williams

Details of Investigation into Underwear Ghost

Date	Action	Reaction
15/9	Duct tape X across front of drawer	Undies removed without apparent movement of the duct tape.
18/9	Loads of duct tape slathered all over the front of the drawer, making it impossible to open drawer without a pair of scissors.	Undies scattered around room. Wad of duct tape still plastered across drawer. Upon opening of drawer, strange cold spot was felt inside drawer where undies usually reside. Remains of spirit?
20/9	Mousetrap hidden in left cup of Wonderbra (worn only on special occasions).	Trap triggered, undies strewn about, but no signs of injured fingers on anyone in the family (suspects: Chris Williams, Dr. Williams, or Bess Williams). Proof that entity has physical interaction with stuff.
25/9	Powdered paint applied to handle of	Not very successful. Hopes were that paint

drawer in case one of the occupants of the house is pulling a fast one.

would dye hands of culprit, but powered paint didn't cling to the brass handle very well unless first wetted, which pretty much defeated the purpose of using powder. Could this be evidence of ghostly interaction?

29/9   Consultation with Rev. Brand Miller, Piddlington-on-the-Weld church.

Rev. Miller refused opportunity to conduct exorcism on underwear drawer, stating it was against Church of England policy to conduct exorcisms. Suggested researching history of house for possible information on ghost known to haunt undie drawer. Research on house history will commence immediately after half-term holiday.

Subject: My day, and you're welcome to it
From: Mrs.Oded@btelecom.co.uk
To: Dru@seattlegrrl.com
Date: 9 October 2003 8:16 pm

I'm glad your date with Weasel-V went well. I don't

blame you at all for not wanting to touch him there. I mean, it's bound to be ooky and all. Did you feel weird when he asked you to touch the WeaselMeister? I think something's wrong with me, Dru, I really do. I mean, I've seen pictures of them, and instead of thinking they look great and all, they just look funny to me. Shouldn't I be thinking they're hot and stuff? Aidan is a hottie hot-hot-hotalicious guy . . . shouldn't I be, like, *happy* that he wanted me to touch him? What if he still wants me to? I think the only way I'm going to be able to touch him *there* is if I'm looking at something else. Maybe it's not me, maybe it's just Aidan. Maybe I should see some others, you know, for comparison.

So I ran into Fang when Mom made me go grocery shopping with her. He's living on his own now, in a student house, which is cool except he looked kind of sad. Aidan said Fang doesn't get along with his dad, so I'm wondering if he left home because of that. He was buying a bunch of frozen stuff and cans of soup, and when I told Mom that he was really nice, she invited him over for dinner. He's going to come Saturday night, then take me to Devon's party after, which will be cool because it'll look like I'm going with him, even though I'm not. Going with him. I mean, I am, but I'm not. Oh, you know what I mean.

Anyway, Mom was off buying fabric softener for her precious towels, so I helped Fang pick out some frozen dinners, and somehow, I mentioned that I was organizing the Vampire Ball.

"Vampire Ball?" he asked, holding a package of frozen fish sticks.

I handed him one of stuffed sole instead. "Yeah, I'm in charge of the Halloween party, and Holly thought it would be cool to do a Vampire Ball, so that's what we're doing. It's going to be major radical, too, because we have Black Death for the band, and there will be prizes for costumes and stuff."

"Costumes? Oh, it's a fancy dress ball." He looked at the stuffed sole.

"It's better for you. More healthy. The fish sticks are loaded with nitrates and stuff."

He grinned and put the sole in his basket. "Thanks. About this Vampire Ball, can anyone go?"

I picked out a package of frozen stuffed peppers. "You like these?" He nodded. I handed them to him and moved down to the next section. "It's only open to Gobottom students and their dates."

"Oh. Are you going with anyone?"

"Um, no." I gnawed on my lip for a second. "Mac and cheese OK?"

He looked at the package. "Sure. Would you like to go to the ball with me?"

Oh, God, he asked me. Think quick, Emily! "OK."

I know, I know! I was waiting for Aidan to ask me, but I've dropped all sorts of hints and he hasn't asked, and I just can't wait any longer. The ball is in less than three weeks, and I have to coordinate my costume with my date's, so I said yes. I just couldn't go by myself, like Peg. She doesn't care at all about her cool rating, but I have my reputation to think of. So I'm going with Fang, which isn't totally horrible, because he is nineteen and has nice eyes and stuff.

"Good," he said.

"Yeah," I said. Honestly, I don't know why I always sound like such a moron around him, but I do. I guess it's 'cause he doesn't feel like a guy, you know? I'm not all worried about making an impression on him or anything, I can just be me with Fang, kind of like how I am with you, only I wouldn't tell him I was having cramps or stuff like that. "What about some turkey?"

He looked at his basket. It was full of frozen food. "I think I have enough for now," he said, and smiled that nice smile at me.

"Oh, sorry, I didn't mean to do that. I guess it's my mom's genes. She likes to feed people. So we'll see you on Saturday."

He grinned even more. "I'm looking forward to eating something that's not been frozen first."

Mom came zipping back down the aisle, so we said good-bye. She grilled me on the way home about Fang, and didn't seem to like the fact that he was nineteen and living on his own, but I told her she was just being Ancient with a capital A, and she needed to get with the times.

Turns out Bess is having her Monk over that night, too, so it should be quite an interesting dinner.

Gotta go. I have to do some work on my paper that explains why Hamlet was really stupid by pretending to be mad (he lost Ophelia). Fill me up with gossip, buttercup!

XXs and OOs,
~Em

Subject: My Life Is Now Officially Over
From: Mrs.Oded@btelecom.co.uk
To: Dru@seattlegrrl.com
Date: 12 October 2003 9:01 am

I know I've said my life is over before, but this time I mean it. I'll never have a life again. I'm not ever stepping foot out of this house. Mom and Brother and Bess will go back home next year, and I'll have to stay with the underwear ghost, because I can't possibly ever face anyone again after what happened last night. I hope the prof that Brother did the job swap with doesn't mind me hanging around until I'm thirty or so. Or dead, whichever comes first.

I'm sorry you're having problems with Vance right now (didn't I *tell* you he would two-time you with Tabitha? And after you went to the trouble of telling him about Viagra!), but this is much, much more important. This is my whole life.

OK, I'm going to do this properly so you can relive the horror with me. First of all, I had a bit of a problem with my makeup. Now, you know that I'm really good at evening makeup—you told me that no one does eyeliner quite like I do. Well, my eyeliner (Ebony Passion) would not go on right. It kept smudging and making big blots. So I took it off and had to use Chestnut Nights, which, as you know, isn't a good color for night because it's not dark enough. That was the first crisis.

Then my dress (the black velvet one with the short skirt and the long chiffon sleeves) had a tear in the armpit, which meant I had to get Mom's sewing kit so I could fix it. Crisis number two.

Then Fang came. The only explanation I can think of for what Brother said is that he's obviously going senile. That, or he's started drinking and no one knows it yet.

"This is Fang Baxter," I said, introducing him to Brother. Mom was out in the kitchen with Bess doing stuff. Bess's BF Monk was slouched in a chair watching

TV. Brother was watching Monk with the same look on his face that he has when Mom makes Brussels sprouts.

"Fang?" he asked, looking even more Brussels sprouty.

"It's actually Francis, but my mates call me Fang," Fang explained. Brother stood up and they shook hands and did that man sort of chat for a couple of minutes before Bess came in and dragged Monk off to the dining room.

"Dinner's on. Hi, you must be Fang. I'm Bess. This is Monk. I hope you like chicken curry, Mom's determined to go British. I told her she needs to come with us to the poultry protest we've got on next week. Do you have any idea of the amount of mercury that's contained in English chickens?"

"She's adopted," I told Fang as we toddled off to the dining room. "I don't share any of her genes."

He laughed.

Everything was fine until the food stopped being passed around, and we started eating. Then the man who claims he is my father started the dinner conversation out by looking over at Fang and asking, "So, do you plan on having sex with my daughter?"

I shot a piece of chicken I was eating out of my nose. I swear to you, it shot out my nose!

"BROTHER!"

"Erm—" Fang looked more than a little startled. He just blinked at Brother, his fork halfway to his mouth. "Eh—"

"Dear, perhaps now is not the best time for this conversation," Mom said.

"Yes!" I said fervently, nodding like mad and wiping my nose. Chicken hurts! "Like, *never!*"

Brother hoisted the Unibrow and looked at Mom.

"She is my daughter. I believe I have the right to know if this young man plans on copulating with her."

"OH MY GOD!" I covered my face with my hands. I couldn't believe my father was doing this to me. How could he hate me so much?

"After all, I know the other one is having sex with Bess; she told me so."

"That's right, isn't it, my little stud muffin?" Bess asked, sliding her hand up Monk's thigh.

"Bess, not at the dinner table. Brother, there is a time and place for this discussion, and it's not while we are eating. This can wait until later." Mom tried again.

Brother eyed Fang carefully. "What do you say, Fang? You planning on getting lucky with Emily?"

I slid off the chair and curled up into a fetal ball on the floor. "Getting lucky? Brother, if you're going to humiliate me like this, the least you can do is not use Old People Slang."

"Humiliate you? I'm not trying to humiliate you; I'm just trying to stay in touch with what's going on in your life. Your mother made a deal with me when you were born. Of course, I didn't know you were going to be asking about Viagra and running around with condoms just waiting to pounce on some boy."

I lay flat out on the floor and prayed for it to open up and suck me in, prayed for a hurricane that would destroy the house instantly, prayed for a bolt of lightning to come down and strike my father dead.

"Actually, I'm not planning on it, Professor Williams," Fang said. "Emily's too young."

I got to my knees and peered over the table at him. "Too young? TOO YOUNG? Just what do you mean by that?"

"Maybe 'young' isn't the right word. I just meant that I'd want you to know me a lot better before we . . . er . . . did anything."

"Smart boy," Brother said, waving a piece of curried chicken at him. "Got a good head on your shoulders. Where did you say you're going to school?"

"Oxfordshire Agricultural College."

"He's going to be a vet; isn't that nice?" Mom said.

I glared at Fang. "Young?"

"Inexperienced?" he asked.

I thought about it for a minute, then got back into my chair. "It's better."

"Good," Brother said, and smiled at Mom. "You see? There's never a wrong time to discuss these things."

I breathed a sigh of relief and picked up my fork. Brother had embarrassed me, but it wasn't a mortal embarrassment. I had survived it, and Fang didn't look shocked anymore.

Suddenly Brother looked up and pointed his fork at Fang again. "You include oral sex in that statement, too, correct? She's too young for that, as well."

"GAH!" I shouted, then grabbed my plate and Fang's. "Come on, Fang, we're going to eat in the library where there are no sex-obsessed deranged old people trying to ruin the shreds of what's left of my life."

Be back in a mo. Have to get some aspirin. Just thinking about last night has made my headache worse.

~Em

Subject: OK, I'm back
From: Mrs.Oded@btelecom.co.uk
To: Dru@seattlegrrl.com
Date: 12 October 2003 9:09 am

I have a head that would kill a normal human, but not me, oh, no—I have to survive so I can relive again and again the horrible calamity of last night.

Where was I? Oh, yeah, the Brother Incident. Fang and I had our dinner in the library, and he actually told me that his dad once threatened to cut off his balls if he got a girl pregnant, so that made me feel better. That I'm not the only one whose father is sex-obsessed, that is, not that Fang's dad threatened to cut off his noogies.

Anyway, we managed to avoid the Sex Fiend for another hour, then off we went to Devon's for the big party.

"I thought you didn't have a car," I said as we got into a ratty little VW. He held the door open for me, which at first I thought was really romantic, until he explained that it had to be closed from the outside, or else the door would pop off.

"It's my mate's," he said, gunning the engine. It died twice. He gave me an apologetic little smile. "It needs a bit of work."

"That's OK. It's awfully nice of you to offer to take me to Devon's."

"My pleasure."

Devon doesn't live too far from us, but in an expensive neighborhood. The houses are all set way back off the road, and surrounded by big stone fences with iron gates. You know, the kind of houses that have *names*.

Devon lived in one called Penhallow, a huge pink stone house with lots of windows and a separate five-car garage. It was really impressive, and I was glad I'd shaved earlier, because it was the sort of place that you don't want to go into with hairy armpits.

"Wow, that's some house," I said as Fang opened the

car door for me.

"Dev's dad is a coroner."

"A coroner?" I asked, smiling to myself when he took my hand. We started up the curved drive toward the front steps. "Isn't that the guy who does stuff with dead bodies?"

"That's right. Dev's dad is a coroner with Scotland Yard. Very important. Gets called in on all the sensitive cases."

"Oh. Cool. I think. You don't think he brings his work home with him, do you?"

Fang laughed and squeezed my hand. "No, I'm sure he doesn't. You're not nervous, are you?"

Oh, God, how did he know? "No, of course not. Why do you ask?"

"Because you're cutting off the circulation in three of my fingers."

"Oh." I loosened my grip on his hand, but I didn't let it go altogether. I'm not stupid! "You should see me when I'm really nervous. You wouldn't be able to feel anything below your elbow."

He laughed again and rang the doorbell. A group of two guys and two girls came up behind us, calling to him as the door opened. Some guy I didn't recognize greeted Fang and waved us in. The hallway was gorgeous, black and white tile on the floor, a big curved wrought iron staircase sweeping up to the floor above (first or second, I can never keep it straight what they call it here), a huge chandelier, and arty stuff like really old-looking pictures and big urns. Doors opened on either side to show huge rooms. Fang took my coat and dropped it off in a small room at the end of the hall, then shooed me into the room on the left.

"Lalla!" I said, a bit relieved that I knew someone besides just Fang. Holly had decided she wasn't up to a "posh party" and stayed home, so I really was on my own. Except for the guys and Lalla and Peg, that is. Fang mumbled something about saying hi to some mates, and went off to talk to a group of guys who were standing in the corner laughing at each other.

Lalla looked up from where she was talking to a friend. "Emily! Oooh, you look ever so nice! That's a stunning brill dress. This is Ronnie."

"Hi, Ronnie. Thanks, Lalla," I said, assuming that "stunning brill" was good. "I like your leather bustier. It's really coolio."

She stood up and turned around so I could see all of it. "It's fabulous, isn't it? Crimson leather. I got it at Garfinkles. Tash got me a discount on it."

Tash. Grr. I knew that since she was Devon's cousin, she was likely to be at the party, but that didn't mean I had to like it. And speaking of Tash . . . "Have you seen Aidan tonight?" I asked, looking around the room. It was pretty crowded, and growing more crowded with each ring of the doorbell. The room on the other side of the hall was just as filled as this one, and I noticed a lot of people had drinks and munchies in their hands.

"He's here somewhere. If I know him, he's probably playing bartender. Why don't you go see? Drinkies and food are just through that door."

"OK. Thanks. Nice meeting you, Ronnie."

I headed off to the huge dining room (I'm thinking forty or fifty people could have fit in it) that had a long, long table covered in food, plates, napkins, etc., and at the end was a portable bar with two guys behind it, pouring out drinks. Neither one was Aidan.

"You all alone, li'l girl?" a guy asked behind me. He plopped his arm down over my shoulder and puffed beery breath in my face. "Jus' say th' word, and ol' Josh'll take care of you, yes, I will. Take care of you. Li'l girls shouldn't be 'lone. 'S very bad thing."

I shrugged my way out from under his arm. "Um, no, I'm here with . . . with . . . Aidan."

"Aid'n? Aid'n? Oh, yeah, bloke in the back snogging the blond bird. You don' want him, li'l girl. He's pro-copied."

"Yes, well, I'd better go find him."

"Repocopied."

"You said he's in the back? That way?"

"Preecopeed."

"Preoccupied, and I'll find him myself."

GOD! Drunks! Ew! I hurried down another hallway, smaller than the first, until I reached the back of the house. People were wandering all around here, too, everyone laughing and drinking and joking with each other. I never knew Devon had so many friends! I looked into each room as I passed it, and at last found Aidan in a room that looked like our library, only much, much nicer. Lots of glossy leather chairs, leather books, dead animal heads on the wall, expensive-looking rugs on the floor, that sort of thing. Aidan was sitting in a big leather armchair with Tash in his lap, leaning over side-ways and laughing at something Devon was saying. Devon, oddly enough, didn't have any girls hanging off him. I was a bit surprised, because he usually always had at least one girl with him, but this time he was by himself. I guess he was being polite, since he was the host.

"Oh, look, there's your little schoolmate," Tash said,

her scratchy voice making my ears hurt.

"Emily!" Devon said, grabbing two drinks from a table and beetling straight for me. He handed me a glass, then leaned forward and kissed me. RIGHT ON THE LIPS!

"Um," I said, trying to look like I greet guys by kissing them all the time. "Hi, Devon. Great party."

"It is now that you're here," he said, half turning to wave his drink at the people in the room. "You know everyone?"

"Um—"

"Good. Drink up, drink up, there's plenty where that came from."

I looked down at the drink. It was clear and had one tiny little sliver of ice and a curl of lemon. "Oh. Thanks. I will. It's just that I'm not really one for . . . um . . . vodka."

"That's a G and T," Devon said.

"Ah. Sure." Whatever. I'd worry about what that was later, right at that moment all I wanted to know was why Aidan hadn't come over to say hi, more explicitly, why he wasn't pushing that scratchy-voiced Tash off his lap.

"Come in, make yourself at home. Aidan's here, but I expect you know that, don't you?" Devon's eyes twinkled when he said that.

"Oh, Dev, don't pick on her. She's so sweet and innocent, I'm sure she doesn't even drink, let alone understand the sort of complex relationship that Aidan and I have. Isn't that right, love?" She kissed Aidan as she said the last part. I waited for a minute to see if he was going to stop her, but he didn't seem to.

It was the last straw, Dru. My heart shattered into a

thousand little itty-bitty pieces. I'd lost Aidan to a she-wolf. There was only one thing left for me to do.

I had to prove that I wasn't sweet and innocent. I had to show Aidan and everyone that I drank and flirted and made out and touched guys and all that kind of stuff. I was through being Miss Responsible. All *that* had ever done was bring me heartache.

I tossed back the drink, choked for a minute on the sliver of ice, then spat out the lemon rind and gasped for air when fire roared down my throat and burst into my stomach.

Devon laughed and patted me on the back. "That's my girl! Another one?"

"Line 'em up," I said, copying a line I'd heard in an old movie. It sounded cool.

The next thing I knew—and I'm being totally honest here—after I saw Tash on Aidan's lap sucking the poor guy's tongue right out of his head, the rest of the evening is kind of spotty in my memory. I do remember Devon hauling me up the big curved staircase, one arm around my waist, laughing and calling down to the people in the hall who were hooting and yelling something up to us.

"Bombs away!" I remember saying as I dropped my drink onto the floor below. Everyone seemed to think that was hilarious, although thinking back on it now, I don't know why. I mean, it was a *glass* glass, and I'm sure it broke and the drink splattered everywhere.

I also remember Devon leaning against me as he pulled me along the upper hall. There were people everywhere up there, too, mostly couples leaning up together against the wall, snogging like mad. Devon had his arm around me, and I wasn't even shocked even though he wasn't my BF! I felt so floaty and a bit twirly that I thought it was perfectly fine that he should be nuzzling my ear, although now that I think about it, ears aren't really that sexy, are they?

"Come to my room, sweetheart," Devon said to me, his eyes bright blue and glistening just like your mom's sapphire ring.

"Sure. Boy, is it hot in here? I'm hot. I'm really really really really really hot."

He sucked on a spot beneath my ear that made me go all boneless and tingly. "Oh, yes, you are hot. I've wanted you to burn me for so long, sweetheart."

"Maybe I have a fever," I said as he opened a door to a room and pushed me inside. "Maybe I have the flu, because you know, not only am I really hot, but my stomach feels a bit woobidy."

He pulled me up against a bed and did the same sort of hands skimming over me move that Aidan had done at the club, only this was much nicer because it was warm. Hot, really. I couldn't imagine why Devon had the house so hot. It was making me sweat, and you know I'm not at my best when I sweat.

"You smell so good," he said, kissing my neck. "I wanted to do this ever since I met you, but I thought you were Aidan's girl. I'm glad you're not."

I got a little sad at that, and made boo-boo lips. "I was Aidan's GF, but he likes Tash better than me. Isn't that sad? I think it's sad. I think it's very very very sad."

"Mmmfrwrf," he said as he nuzzled my collarbone, which made me sadder because Aidan didn't want to mmmfrwrf into my collarbone.

"Hey!" I said, suddenly realizing just what was happening. I was with Devon! And he was kissing me! I was in love with Aidan, but I was kissing Devon. In his bedroom! OHMIGOD! "Hey! Hey! HeeeeeeEEEEEEEEEEEEEEEE!"

His tongue slipped past my lips into my mouth. It touched my tongue! It was so weird! On the one hand, I really liked French kissing Devon, because he was a much better kisser than Aidan, but on the other hand, I didn't love Devon, and I did love Aidan, and isn't it a major sin to like kissing a guy you're not in love with more than kissing the one you do love? It was all so confusing, I didn't know what to do, so I kissed him back for a little bit.

If I hadn't been so hot, and my stomach hadn't been so woobidy, I think I might really have gotten into it despite the fact that he wasn't my BF, but all of a sudden the really nice feeling of kissing him changed into something not so nice, and grew and grew until I thought I was going to barf.

And then I did. All over Devon.

I woke up lying on his bed, something cold touching my face. It felt so good, I leaned into it, wanting more. "Hot," I said, that horrible barf aftertaste in my mouth. My tongue felt like it had been dipped in wax.

The cold thing went away, then came back again, wetter and colder. I pried open my eyes and saw that it was a washcloth, and thought, for some stupid reason, that part of the problem with England was that the stuff they call things just doesn't make sense.

"It's a washcloth, not a flannel. I don't know why they call it a flannel," I said, a little startled that I spoke out loud what I was thinking.

"Is that so?" a familiar voice asked. I turned my head and saw Fang. It was his hand at the end of the washcloth.

156 ▶

"What are you doing here?" I asked. Well, "croaked" might be a better word to describe my voice. My throat burned and I tried to not speak at him, because I was sure I had barf breath, and I'd just die if he knew I barfed on Devon.

"Dev asked me to come up. He's changing his clothes."

Oh, God, he knew!

"Gah!" I tried to scream, but it came out a kind of gargled moan. Then I remembered what Devon had been doing before I barfed on him and pushed back the washcloth to check myself. There weren't any visible signs that he had kissed me, no big blinking neon sign over my head that read *Has Enjoyed French Kissing Boy Who Is Not Her Boyfriend*, or anything else like that. At least I didn't have to live through the shame of having Fang know Devon was trying to get busy with me when I barfed on him. "I'm sick. I think I have the flu."

Fang didn't even smile. He just put his hand on the back of my neck. "I don't think so."

"I am too. I'm hot and I threw up. That's sick."

"No, that's pissed," Devon said, coming out of another room. I suddenly realized that I was lying down on a bed, his bed, which meant I was in his bedroom. With him! And I'd barfed on him! After he'd sucked on my tongue!

"OHMIGOD, I just want to die."

"Yep, she's pissed all right." Devon's voice was kind of muffled because Fang was cold washclothing me again.

"I'm not mad, I'm sick," I told the washcloth. Fang pulled it away.

"All right to sit up now?" he asked. I couldn't look him in the eye. It was too mortifying. He knew I'd barfed. God take me now, because my life is over.

"I'm OK, just sick."

"You going to take her home?" Fang asked Devon.

"I would, but if I leave, who knows what will happen to the house?"

I tried to sit up, but the room kept spinning and making my stomach flip-flop, so I lay back down and prayed for death.

"You should have thought about that before you poured all that booze into her."

"How was I to know she couldn't hold it? She had a hollow leg, Fang, you should have seen her tossing back those G and Ts. I thought she was used to it."

"She's probably never drunk hard alcohol before, you idiot."

"I have so," I said, trying not to breathe (it made my stomach worse). "I drink wine every Christmas, and Dru and I had a lovely Mai Tai party when her mom went to Aspen."

There was silence for a minute. "Can't you take her home for me, Fang?"

"I guess I'm going to have to, aren't I?"

I wanted to cry. There I was sick and no one wanted to take me home. I was worse than miserable, I was pathetic.

There was a sound like someone sighing heavily, then Fang said, "Go get Trev's car, you know which one it is. Bring it round back. I'll take her down the back stairs so no one will see her. Maybe she's so pissed she won't remember any of this."

"Thanks, mate. I owe you for this."

"More than you know. What do you think her parents are going to have to say?"

Why were they going on about me being pissed? Somewhere in the dim, foggy depths of my mind I remembered that "pissed" meant "drunk."

"I'm not drunk. I'm sick," I said again, suddenly really tired. I couldn't keep my eyes open I was so tired. Things got a bit woozy again then, but I do remember Fang picking me up and carrying me, because it made my stomach lurch around. Then there was wonderfully cold air, and I could sleep some more, and then Mom and Brother were talking, and Fang was saying something, but I couldn't quite understand him because he sounded like he was talking into a tin can.

I threw up again, sometime in the middle of the night, but at least I made it to the bathroom for that. When I woke up this morning, I thought I had died and was in hell. My mouth tasted like . . . well, I can't even think of anything bad enough to describe it. My head hurt. My eyeballs hurt. My hair hurt. I felt like I was made out of something really, really fragile, and I had stress fractures all over and was about to shatter.

Gah. I need more aspirin. The ones I took aren't working. Be back in a couple of minutes.

~Em

Subject: I think my head is going to explode
From: Mrs.Oded@btelecom.co.uk
To: Dru@seattlegrrl.com
Date: 12 October 2003 10:51 am
I feel SO AWFUL. I can't even begin to tell you how awful I feel, except to say that the air around me is too thick. I can't breathe it in. It won't fit into my lungs.

Let's see, where was I . . . oh, yeah, this morning. By

the time I staggered to the bathroom, I realized what had happened. Devon and Fang were right: I had been drunk. I couldn't even imagine what they must be thinking about me, it made my brain hurt too much, but I do know this—I will never be able to face either of them again. Ever. I just can't do it. I would scream, except then my head would splat open and it's not fair to Mom to make her clean up the brain-splat mess.

My eyelashes are way too heavy.

So I managed to brush my teeth (I swore they screamed when I touched them) and my tongue and the rest of my mouth to get that lovely après-barf taste out of it, and then I staggered downstairs to face up to the Lecture of a Lifetime. I figured I'd get it over with as quickly as possible, since my whole body was kind of numb around the edges, and it would be better to have the lecture when I didn't actually have the ability to hear it.

"Ah, Emily," Brother said, looking over the *Sunday Post* to cock the Unibrow at me. "There you are. You look ghastly. Doesn't she look ghastly, Chris?"

Mom was pouring herself a cup of coffee. The molecules of coffee in the air pounded my body. I almost fell over. "Yes, yes, she does. She looks as if she feels like she's been turned inside out. I can't imagine it's a good feeling."

"Gah," I said, and sort of slumped into a chair.

"I remember feeling as if a herd of elephants had danced on me once," Brother said. "It was the time I went to South America and got malaria, but even after lying in bed with a fever for two weeks, I believe I looked much better than Emily does. Have you noticed the fact that the flesh around her eyes is red and swollen to the point you can hardly see her eyes?"

I tried to gingerly feel around one eye to see how much Brother was exaggerating, but instead of an eye my fingers found two big sausage rolls of flesh with a few eyelashes poking through them, so I decided it was better that I not explore any further.

"I did notice that. And the green pallor of her skin— would you say it had the same consistency and color tone that a week-old dead frog has?"

I touched my cheek. It felt green.

Brother tipped his head as he considered my frog flesh. "Oh, I don't know. You remember that dead body they found in the Green River? The one that had been in there six months? I think her skin tone looks more like that than a dead frog."

"Gark."

"The bits that remained, of course. So much of the corpse was eaten off by fish."

I tried to stand, but couldn't get my legs to work. "You're both cruel. Why can't you just lecture me and ground me like any other parents? Why do you have to make this worse?"

Mom smiled her evil mom smile. "What are you talking about, dear?"

"I believe she's speaking of the fact that she was brought home last night in a near stupor, smelling of vomit and alcohol, having passed out earlier, according to the young man into whose hands we had placed the responsibility for her safety and well-being, a responsibility he had obviously failed to keep."

Oh, God, what had he said to Fang? I wanted to die all over again. "No one is responsible for my safety and well-being but me," I muttered, trying to think of how I was going to apologize to Fang, since I wasn't ever going to be able to face him again.

"I'm glad to hear that you recognize that fact," Brother said dryly.

"Fang didn't do anything wrong."

The Unibrow rose in question. "He didn't," I said stubbornly, then instantly regretted it as a red wave of pain washed over me. I took a very slow, very gentle deep breath, and figured I'd better get it over with. The Parentals weren't going to let me go without admitting the worst. "It was all my fault. I was trying to prove something, and . . . well . . . I didn't."

"Ah," Brother said. That was all. Just "Ah."

It was hard to see him clearly through the swollen eye sausages, but I could see enough to recognize that he was wearing his smug look. "What are you going to do to me?"

The Unibrow did a little up-and-down motion that instantly made me seasick. "What do you mean, what are we going to do to you?"

"Punishment," I said, hating to say it, but figuring I couldn't possibly be more miserable than I was at that moment.

Mom laughed again, a horrible, harsh sound that scraped across my brain like shards of glass. "I think you've been punished enough, Emily."

I tried to blink, but my eyelashes got tangled up in the sausages. "You're not going to do anything?"

She shook her head.

"Oh." I thought about it for a minute with the part of my mind that was still functioning. "I'm supposed to have learned something from this, aren't I?"

They both nodded.

"'K. Can I learn it later, after my eyes stop bleeding?"

"Your eyes aren't bleeding, Em."

"They feel like they are." I stood up very slowly and, clutching the available bits of furniture, made my way to the library, where the air molecules were slightly less dense.

Poop, phone. Must be Holly checking on me to see how the party went. Gah. BRB.

. . .

Oh, God. Oh, God. OOOOOOOOOOH, GOOOOOOOOOOD. That was Holly, only she wasn't calling to ask me about the party—she was calling to tell me to get dressed in my coolest outfit, because she and her stepdad are coming by in half an hour to pick me up to go to some hospital for terminally ill kids where Oded is doing pictures and signing autographs! AAAAAAAAAAAAAAAAAAAAAAAAAAAGH! My one chance to meet him and he's going to see me with week-old dead-frog, corpse-like flesh and sausage eye rolls! I WANT TO DIE.

Must go. Must meet Oded. Must apply massive quantities of makeup.

I hope I survive the walk up the stairs.

Hs and Ks,
~Em

Subject: I could just die
From: Mrs.Oded@btelecom.co.uk
To: Fbaxter@oxfordshire.agricoll.co.uk
CC: Dru@seattlegrrl.com
Date: 12 October 2003 5:40 pm

Fang, I'm really, really, really sorry that you had to take me home on Saturday. You really were nice to do it, especially since I seem to remember drooling on the door of your friend's car on the way home. I hope there wasn't a lot to clean up. I'm also really sorry that you had to explain to Brother what happened. I hope he didn't yell at you or anything.

Anyway, since I am too embarrassed to ever see you or Devon again, will you please have a really nice life? I'm sorry I was such an idiot.

Emily

Subject: Re: Don't worry about it
From: Mrs.Oded@btelecom.co.uk
To: Fbaxter@oxfordshire.agricoll.co.uk
CC: Dru@seattlegrrl.com
Date: 12 October 2003 5:50 pm

Fbaxter wrote:
> *Don't be silly. You don't have anything to be*
> *embarrassed about. I think everyone needs to get*
> *really legless once, just so you know how bad it feels.*

Well, I'm glad you aren't thinking the worst of me because I got ripped, but the fact still remains that I can't see you again. I hope your vet stuff goes well.

Emily

Subject: Re: You're making too much about nothing
From: Mrs.Oded@btelecom.co.uk
To: Fbaxter@oxfordshire.agricoll.co.uk
CC: Dru@seattlegrrl.com
Date: 12 October 2003 5:56 pm

Fbaxter wrote:
> *believe me, you'll get over it. I always did, and I did*
> *worse things than get pissed and pass out. Besides,*
> *I'm taking you to the Vampire Ball. You have to see*
> *me, at least one more time.*

I've changed my mind. Good-bye. I hope you have a
really happy life.

Emily

Subject: Re: Sorry
From: Mrs.Oded@btelecom.co.uk
To: Fbaxter@oxfordshire.agricoll.co.uk
CC: Dru@seattlegrrl.com
Date: 12 October 2003 5:58 pm

Fbaxter wrote:
> *I'm taking you, and that's that. What sort of a fancy*
> *dress am I supposed to wear?*

You can't come. Go away.

Emily

Subject: Re: Do you want to go see the new James Bond?
From: Mrs.Oded@btelecom.co.uk
To: Fbaxter@oxfordshire.agricoll.co.uk
CC: Dru@seattlegrrl.com
Date: 12 October 2003 5:59 pm

Fbaxter wrote:
> *I'm no different than I was before, and I certainly*
>*don't think any less of you, you daft girl!*

Well . . . OK. You can take me to the Vampire Ball, but you can't look at me. Ever. Those are my conditions.

Emily

P.S. I can't see the Bond, James Bond, on Friday or Sat, but I'm free on Sunday. Is that OK with you?

Subject: Re: Will you guys stop e-mailing me?
From: Mrs.Oded@btelecom.co.uk
To: Dru@seattlegrrl.com
Date: 12 October 2003 11:39 pm

Dru wrote:
> *Will you guys take me off this loop? I don't care*
> *whether or not you go see the new James Bond*
> *movie (it's really cool—you're going to love it) or not.*
> *I have stuff to do. I can't keep reading your e-mails!*
> *Dru*
>
> *P.S.—Em, e-mail me full details.*

What stuff do you have to do? Tell all. Are you still mad at me about Oded?

Hugs and kisses,
~Em

Subject: Re: AAAAAUGH!
From: Mrs.Oded@btelecom.co.uk
To: Dru@seattlegrrl.com
Date: 15 October 2003 3:38 pm

Dru wrote:
> *coolest picture I have ever seen! You didn't look*
> *puffy or corpse-like at all—you looked fabu,*
> *utterly fabu! I'm so jealous! I can't believe you told*
> *him you would be able to legally marry him if your*
> *parents gave their permission! I JUST CAN'T BELIEVE*
> *YOU GOT TO MEET ODED! I would have died!*

What can I say, my life occasionally has its moments. Unfortunately, those moments are darned few and far between. This week has been hellish (with the exclusion of showing EVERYONE the picture of Oded hugging me). The Duff turned me in for skipping the last two classes on Monday (I had to go get copies made of the Oded picture, didn't I?), which means I have to sweep out the girls' locker room for *two weeks!* Sucky, huh? I mean, these people are taking school way too seriously!

Madame Grayson finally figured out what I was doing in French. I think it was the claim of tuberculosis that did it, but I'm not sure. It might have been the glandular fever I was supposed to have had last week. Anyway, I had to go see Russell Crowe.

"Mrs. Grayson tells me that you've not been participating in French," Mr. Krigon said, all nice and friendly-like. He was sitting on the edge of his desk with one leg propped up, and I would have gone all girly about that, but honestly, I was just too tired. My life has just become too complicated lately to have the energy left over to lust after Russell Crowe look-alikes. After all, I kissed Oded! How can I accept anything less than one hundred percent authentic after that?

"Um, well . . . that would probably be . . . " I tried to get my brain to think of a reason I couldn't talk in French, but it wasn't working. I think I've burned out something. I decided I'd better just spill. "The truth is, I don't know any French."

He arched his eyebrows up in surprise. "You don't know any French?"

I nodded. "None. Nada. Zip. Zilcho—"

"I get the idea, Emily." He looked grim for a moment, then his lips started to twitch. "Tuberculosis?"

I couldn't help it. I giggled. "Too much, do you think?"

He gave in and laughed, shaking his head as he did. "Too much. Ah, Emily, what are we going to do with you?"

"Put me in the sixth form where I belong?" I asked hopefully.

He shook his head again. "We've had this talk before. I realize that you're ahead of the fifth form students in age, and it's true you're doing exceptionally well in your classes—all but French—but I can't justify violating the rules just to salve your ego."

"I'm not fitting in very well with the fifth form," I pointed out. "I'm sure I wouldn't have any problems in the sixth. Miss Naylor is giving me sixth form work in physics now—"

"I'm sorry, Emily, it's just not feasible. Now, about your French problem . . . "

Gah. He's assigned me a tutor from one of the fourth form students. I get a crash course in French, oh, lucky me. He says I have to stay in the French class, but they'll take into consideration my lack of skills. Ha! Like it's my fault? Sheesh! At least I don't have to continue trying to cough up my lung in class.

As if all that weren't bad enough, there was the problem of seeing Aidan. It took me a while to decide what I was going to do about him, and I decided that polite, but rather chilly was good. After all, it's not his fault that he fell victim to the Mouth Leech, although I didn't see him struggling against her very much.

I saw him at lunch on Monday. Holly was out sick, so I had to go over to our table by myself.

"Hi, guys," I said, über-cool and not in the least bit looking like I wanted to rip Aidan's lips off his face and stomp them into the ground. "What's up?"

"Emily!" Aidan jumped up and grabbed my backpack, so I could set my lunch (a salad, thank God) down. "I didn't see you this morning in the library."

He was looking for me? Why? "Um. I was in talking to Mr. Krigon."

He smiled at me, really smiled, with his eyes and mustache and everything. "Trouble?"

"Not really, no."

"Good. I thought you might like to come with me to the Polo Club again. Friday?"

I stared at him, wondering what happened. Two nights ago he was playing sucky-face with Tash, and now he was smiling at me and holding my backpack for me, and asking me out to the Polo Club. I'll never understand men.

"That sounds like fun, but I can't. I'm going to London with my folks after school on Friday. They're going to see a show, and I'm going to buy my costume for the Vampire Ball on Saturday; then we're coming home."

His grin got really big then. It made me go all warm and fuzzy inside. "Why don't you stay home, instead? I'd be happy to keep you company if you are . . . *lonely*."

He was propositioning me! *Me!* Right in front of Lalla and Peg! I fought back a blush and poked at my salad, peeking at the other two to see what they thought. Lalla was talking to the person on the other side of her, but Peg was frowning at Aidan, which was unusual, because Peg really liked Aidan, despite the fact that she doesn't like guys. Sexually, I mean.

"Um . . ." What was I supposed to say? Here was the man of my dreams, Mr. Perfect, Mr. Number One of All-time Hotties, and he was telling me he wanted me. *That way.* "Um . . . well, the truth is, I really have to go to London to get my costume, and since the ball is only a couple of weeks away, and we have all those tests before the half-term break, I think I'll have to go with my parents. Maybe we could . . . um . . . another time?"

"Sure," he said, putting his hand over mine and squeezing my fingers, crushing the little package of croutons I was about to open and put on my salad. "Whenever you like. Just let me know. What about Sunday?"

Sunday? For sex? Was he making a sex date? ACK! I looked over at Peg. She was crunching a celery stick and watching me closely. "Sunday?"

"Maybe we could go to the cinema?"

Sunday. James Bond. Fang. "Oh, sorry, I can't. I'm going . . . " Maybe it wasn't a good idea to tell him I was going out on a date with Fang, even though it wasn't a *date* date—it was just Fang, and just a movie. Then again, maybe it wouldn't hurt. " . . . to see the new James Bond with Fang."

"Ah." His eyes got all squinty for a minute, then he smiled again, and rubbed his fingers over the top of my hand. "Busy girl! Well, there is one thing I know I can do—I can take you to the Vampire Ball."

"Oh," I said, my hand burning up under his fingers. "That would be nice."

I know what you're thinking. I know now. I didn't know then, because my mind was too busy trying to decide what his change to a Hunkable Aidan again meant.

"Good. I thought I'd go as a fallen angel."

I stared at him, my mouth hanging just a little bit open for a second before I realized it was doing that. "OHMIGOD! *I'm* going as a fallen angel! I have the costume all picked out—I found it on-line! I was telling Peg about it last Friday, wasn't I, Peg?"

"Yes," she drawled, back to frowning at Aidan.

"What a coincidence," he said, his eyes kind of shining at me. "I guess it was just meant to be."

Honestly, Dru, it was so romantic, him there stroking my hand, smiling at me, looking at me like he was seeing something new and exciting, not the same old me he'd known for the last month and a half. That's the only reason I can think of that I didn't immediately spot the two flaws to the otherwise perfect plan of us going to the Vamp Ball as fallen angels—the first being that I'd already told Fang I was going with him, the second being the issue of Tash the Face Sucker.

Poop, gotta run, Brother has to upload something this instant or he'll supernova.

Yack at you later.

Hugs and kisses,

~Em

Subject: Raaaaaaavishing!
From: Mrs.Oded@btelecom.co.uk
To: Dru@seattlegrrl.com
Date: 19 October 2003 6:53 pm

I'm baaaaaaaaack! Did you miss me? I wanted to e-mail you last night, but there was a storm and the phones were all wonky, and we got back late, and then today I had to get ready to go on my date with Fang, and model my costume for Holly, and then, of course, I had to get the Lecture from Mom just one more time.

What lecture? Well, here's the poop: When we were in London, Mom and Brother went off to see some boring Old-People play that didn't have any music or anything in it. I stayed in my room for a bit (Brother sprang for a suite, which I thought was cool until I realized that they were flirting with each other, which meant they would be having Parent Sex while we were there, and that just put me right off my dinner). Then Bess went off to go visit some group of radicals, and I figured I might as well check out the hotel. Mom had told me I couldn't go sight-seeing by myself at night, that I had to stay in the hotel or go with Bess, which is just SO unfair! I mean, how can two years make her so much more adult that she can go wandering around while I have to stay put?

Yeah, you're right. Even though they said they're not punishing me for getting drunk at Devon's party, they are.

So anyway, I sat in the lobby for a bit looking very cool and wondering if some handsome sheikh would fall madly in love with me and want to carry me off to wherever, but that got old soon, because the only people in the hotel were ugly and ancient. That's when I noticed that there was a hair salon just off the lobby. How perfect could that be?

I went in and talked to one of the ladies there, and she said she could fit me in then for a coloring and highlight. So I sat down with a book of fake hair snippets and picked out a color I liked (you're going to die, it's *so* fabu!), and while she did it, I tried to figure out how I was going to explain a huge hair charge on Mom's Visa when I'm only supposed to be buying my costume.

The color—it's called Copper Sunset Splendor—came out better than the fake hair sample. It's bright and shiny and the woman did a separate semipermanent color rinse over the top which makes it *outstandingly* gorgeous. I had to change my makeup, since what went with dishwater blond wouldn't go with Copper Sunset Splendor (I found a really deep red lipstick called Rubiyat that looks great on me). Of course, I didn't let Brother or Mom see me that night, but I was majorly cool when I strolled into the sitting room of the suite the next morning. Bess was there alone, reading a newspaper.

"So, what do you think?" I asked her.

"I think the world is going to hell," she answered, her nose still stuck in the paper.

"No, what do you think about my hair?"

She looked up. Her eyes widened. "You look like Lucille Ball."

"I do not!"

"You look like you'd be right at home as Lucy's double."

"I DO NOT!"

She stood up and walked around me, examining all sides of my head. "I'll be damned. You went and dyed your hair orange."

"It's not orange, it's copper. Copper Sunset Splendor! It's *chic!*"

"Um-hmm. Well, if you were looking to have hair that can be seen in the dark, you certainly succeeded."

Honestly, I swear she *is* adopted! I ignored her and went to a chair that faced the door to Mom and Brother's bedroom. It took me a couple of minutes to get a pose that looked both elegant and sophisticated, and yet wholly natural, but at last I did.

"Mom's going to pitch a fit."

"No, she won't," I lied, knowing full well she would, but not caring. I was sixteen. I was old enough to dye my hair if I wanted to. I'd just have to pay her back out of my savings. So what, it just means I don't get that snowboard that I've been eyeing. "She will realize that I'm no longer a child, and she can't tell me what to do with my own body. She let me get my ears pierced, after all."

"That's only because you threatened to quit school if she didn't say yes."

"So?"

"And you didn't get them all done at once. It took you eight months to get them all. Mom didn't notice until you got the last one."

"I don't care. She's not going to mind. She'll open up the door and—" The door to The Parentals' room opened up. Mom stopped in the doorway, took a good long look at me and my Copper Sunset Splendor, then turned around and closed the door again. "—say . . . um . . . that was kind of weird, don't you think?"

"*She what?*" came the muffled cry from the bedroom.

"That was Brother," Bess pointed out.

"I heard," I said, making mean eyes at her.

"Doesn't sound like he's going to be too happy with the new you, either."

I started gnawing on my lip. Maybe I should have warned them about it first.

"If I were you, I'd start thinking up reasons they shouldn't shave your head, because you know Brother; he's going to go—"

"EMILY MARIE WILLIAMS!"

"—ballistic."

Brother stood in the doorway of the bedroom, his eyes bulging out and steam coming from his ears. Well, OK, there wasn't really any steam, but I bet it was only because he hadn't thought of it.

He stared at me for a minute, then turned back to where Mom was lurking behind him. "Dear God, she looks like she should be starring in *I Love Lucy.*"

"Gah!" I shouted, and immediately disowned them all.

So, anyway, we're home now. Fang liked my hair—he said it was very colorful, and now he could pick me out of a crowd just by the glow around my head, which was a nice thing to say, don't you think? We went to the James Bond movie, but didn't do much else because we both had work to do. Fang is working part-time at a stable with the vet there, and one of the pregnant horses is due to pop at any minute, so he has to carry around a beeper in case it goes into labor. I think it sounds kind of ooky and gross, but he says it's not.

Oh! I forgot to tell you! One of the sixth form guys named Glenn asked me out! I don't know him very well, but Holly says he's brutal on the rugby field. I didn't think it's fair to Aidan that I accept, so I told him maybe we could do a movie or something during the half-term break.

That's what's new with me. I'll e-mail you the picture of my costume just as soon as Bess comes back with the digital camera (she's off for a couple of days doing some art project in the north of England). What's going on in your battle to best Tabitha the Trollop? How did you get Connie to tell Vance that Tab had an STD? Did you have to sacrifice your soul or something? Last I heard you told Connie she had a face like a Labrador retriever, and she said your hair smelled like seaweed, and now she's helping you? SPILL!

Hugs and Copper Sunset Splendor kisses,
~Em

Subject: Re: Life Sucks!
From: Mrs.Oded@btelecom.co.uk
To: Dru@seattlegrrl.com
Date: 21 October 2003 4:02 pm

Dru wrote:
> and I'll never get this stupid cast off! There go all
> my chances at a medal this year! How can I possibly
> stay on the team when I won't be able to swim for
> at least six more weeks? I HATE THIS CAST! I HATE
> MY LIFE! It ruined everything, swimming and Vance
> and everything!

Whoa, you are having a bad day! I think you're going through Weasel Withdrawal. Tell you what—go down to the highway and hang around the sleazy strip clubs. There's weasels aplenty there, and one of them ought to make you feel at home.

KIDDING! Honestly, Dru, I don't know what to say. If you've still got it that bad for Vance, well, then you should be fighting for him. Maybe he just doesn't realize how serious you are. I think you should invite him over for dinner, let him do the polite chatty thing with your mom, then drag him off to the den and watch movies. You liked that before, and you said he had a good time. Maybe he needs to be shown that there's more to you than just a really hot babe who happens to have a cast on her foot.

> You never told me what happened when you saw
> Devon. I know you felt bad about Fang, but you
> didn't actually ralph up on him. Have you seen him
> yet? What did you say? What did HE say?

I saw him yesterday, as a matter of fact. I meant to mention it, but I forgot. Holly and I were at the chemist's (drugstore, remember?) buying some glitter fingernail polish for the Vamp Ball, and Devon and some girl I'd never seen before came in.

"OHMIGOD," I said to Holly as I saw them walk past the end of the aisle. "Duck!"

"What?" Holly said as I pulled her down until we were just barely peering over the top of the aisle. "What's wrong?"

"It's Devon," I hissed, and crab-walked down the aisle so I could peek around the end. "And a girl. I don't recognize her."

Devon and the dark-haired girl (pretty, waist-length hair, vinyl skirt, black leather jacket, cool but not quite coolio) headed straight for the aisle that had pads and tampons and . . .

"Condoms!" I said.

"What?" Holly stood up and looked. I pulled her back down and we crouch-walked over a couple of aisles, squatting behind a stack of carrying baskets to watch them.

"They're buying condoms. That or pads, and since she doesn't look bloaty or anything, I bet it's condoms. Well! If that's the way he wants to be, fine!"

"What're you going to do?" Holly whispered.

I thought for a minute, then peeked around the baskets again to make sure Devon was still condom shopping. "Should I pretend I don't know he's there, and if he sees me, act like I don't know him? Or should I just leave and come back later? Or should I act like nothing happened and stroll down the aisle and look surprised to see him?"

"You have to talk to him sometime—he's your boyfriend's best friend."

"Aidan isn't officially my boyfriend," I said, also in a whisper. "He's on probation."

"Yes, but wouldn't it be nicer if you could be around Devon without feeling strange?"

"That's easy for you to say, you've never had his tongue in your mouth. How on earth am I supposed to look someone in the face when I know they've tasted my mouth?"

"That's true. I guess I would feel strange around him, too."

"You see my dilemma," I said, and checked to see what Devon was up to. The condom aisle was empty.

"Rats!"

"What?"

"They're gone."

"Oh. Good, that means I can stand up. I'm getting a cramp in my leg crouching like this."

"Who're you looking for?" a man's voice behind my shoulder whispered.

I shrieked and fell backward onto my butt, looking up to find Devon squatting behind me.

"Sorry, didn't mean to startle you, but when I saw you hiding from someone, I thought I'd offer my assistance. Is it someone from school?"

I shot Holly a look as I got to my feet. "Um . . . yeah. It's no one important."

"Ah." He eyed me up and down, then winked as he wrapped one of my curls around his finger. "You look much better than the last time I saw you. I like the hair; it glows. I guess we get to call you Ginger now."

OHMIGOD! The last time he saw me? The last time he saw me his tongue was doing the tango with my tongue! My face turned bright red, I just know it did, because Holly's eyes got really big when she looked at me. "Um . . . "

He let go of my hair. "I'm glad you're feeling better. That was a killer party, wasn't it? I had a buzz for days. So did Pier, didn't you, sweetheart?"

The dark-haired girl gave him a crooked smile. "You always do throw the wildest parties, Devon. I passed out before I made it back to my flat."

I stared at her for a couple of seconds, wondering if it was normal for people to pass out after they'd been to one of Devon's parties. If so, it would make me feel just a little bit better about the whole horrible evening.

"This is Pier," Devon said, introducing her. "That's Holly, and this is Emily, who can outdrink a sailor when it comes to G and Ts. Well, ladies, we have to be on our way. Pier has promised to give me a massage, haven't you?" He growled into her neck and made her giggle, then wiggled his eyebrows at Holly and me, and left.

I let out a breath I didn't know I was holding. "Hoo!"

"You talked to him," Holly said, her eyes still round. "You talked to a guy you French kissed! And he had another girl with him!"

I straightened up my shoulders and adopted my supercool nonchalant expression (ten out of ten for style) and went back to the glitter fingernail polish. "Yes, well, we both know that Devon's the kind of flirty guy who likes girls a lot. He always seems to have one with him, anyway. And even though he did snog me really thoroughly, I don't care if he has a GF because I'm kind of with Aidan and all."

I don't think Holly bought my supercool nonchalant act, but she didn't say anything else, so I didn't have to confess that I was nervous as a nun in a sex shop around him.

> And speaking of Fang, what are you going to do
> about the party? Are you going to tell Fang
> or Aidan the bad news? How are you going to say
> it, and aren't you worried that one of them is going
> to end up pissed at you?

Geez, I really am forgetting things lately. It must be living with Brother that's making me prematurely senile.

Holly and I worked the Aidan/Fang situation out—I'm going with *both* of them. See, I was worried about hurting Fang's feelings. He was so nice about taking me home the night of the Incident, and I do like him and I don't want to hurt him, which means I can't break it off with him. But Aidan is just so scrummy and nummy and kissalicious, I don't want to miss the chance of seeing whether or not he really is Mr. Emily, so I can't break that date, either. I talked with Holly, and she's agreed to help me by dancing with whoever I'm not dancing with. You know how it is at those kinds of parties—everyone is mingling and dancing and talking and stuff, and half the time you never get to dance with the guy you came with anyway, so I'm sure neither of them will notice. It'll be just fine, trust me.

Oh! You know how everyone in my family keeps mocking my very tight hair color? Well, another of the sixth form guys, Edward, asked me to go clubbing with him. I haven't talked to him much, just seen him in the library and in the IT room, but he seems nice. I was tempted to take him up on the offer, since he's got a really sexy dimple in his chin, but I just couldn't face Aidan if he found out I was seeing someone else on the side. But two guys in a couple of days—that has to be a sign that it's my hair sucking them in, right? I should have dyed it *years* ago. Just think of all the boyfriends I would have had by now!

And speaking of my hair, I have to run. For some reason I'm shedding a lot, big handfuls of hair each day, so I'm going to the Leading Edge (a hair place in POTW) to get some good shampoo. Try not to worry too much about Vance. Weasels always come home to roost.

Hugs and kissy-poos,
~Em

Subject: OHMIGOD!
From: Mrs.Oded@btelecom.co.uk
To: Dru@seattlegrrl.com
Date: 21 October 2003 7:17 pm

The woman at the Leading Edge says it isn't my sham-poo—it was the hair dye! It was too harsh or something and stripped something or burned something or I don't know what, I couldn't listen to her explain it, because it doesn't matter. All that matters is that I'M GOING BALD! Aaaaaaaaack! This is a thousand times worse than Brother talking to Fang about oral sex! The hair woman said I shouldn't dye my hair again for a long time, which means I'm going to have roots and it'll look awful and what am I going to do?

~Em

Subject: Chat room
From: Mrs.Oded@btelecom.co.uk
To: Dru@seattlegrrl.com
Date: 23 October 2003 4:02 pm

Dru wrote:
> I think the best thing is to cut it really short, and then
> have it cut again once the roots start to show. That
> way people will be used to you having short hair
> and they won't think anything of it. Besides, your
> hair is so curly, I bet it would look really good short.

Good? GOOD? Are you insane? Dru, I look like one of those gacky Cabbage Patch dolls with my hair cut short! It makes my nose look too short, and gives me chipmunk cheeks, and you know full well I've been cursed with the Williams Forehead, which I couldn't possibly bare so everyone could see it. I'd die if people saw my forehead, and you can't have a short cut with bangs and chipmunk cheeks without looking like a geek. The only thing for me to do is to start buying hats now, because that's all I'll be able to wear once the rest of my Copper Sunset Splendor falls out.

Mom said she'd pay for me to have it colored my original color of blech, but the Leading Edge woman said she didn't think that would be such a good idea, so it's all over as far as I'm concerned. I told Brother that he could go ahead and give me the money he's paying to the school, because once my hair falls out, I'm never leaving the house again. He just read me a lecture about folly and stupid stuff like that, which I didn't pay any attention to because you know how he is. Honestly, the man is positively *antiquated*.

Well, the big news other than the fact that I'm going bald is that we *finally* got the chat room up and functioning. I think it was a big success, there were lots of kids there, and I heard that the URL was sent out to other schools, so we should have a lot of people in the room. The school put a limit on the time the room is open (after school until midnight, and on the weekends from eight in the morning until midnight), which is a bit sucky, but I'll work on them pushing the hours back. I mean, who goes to bed before midnight on the weekend?

Now, you know the sort of chat room our school has

(had . . . has . . . what*ever!*)—this one is like that, only the people here are so into their texting language that you can't understand them. So instead of saying something even remotely human, they all talk in text language. I did a copy-and-paste from part of the chat tonight to show you what I mean (I'm Skipley, BTW):

Pinkfluffyhandcuffs: u fancy me?

Maximus: fancy who?

R-O-M-E-O: how r ya?

Pinkfluffyhandcuffs: not bad cud b better

Docman: my throat is hurty

Throbbing_Gristle: Skip, I wan u 2 know dat our friendship means a lot 2 me.

Maximus: who fancies u?

Skipley: Um. OK, TG. That's nice. Maximus, who are you asking?

[Lil_Miss_Naughty entered the room.]

Docman: boring bean.

Skipley: Huh?

Throbbing_Gristle: U cry i cry. U laf i laf. Skip.

Lil_Miss_Naughty: any1 wanna snog?

R-O-M-E-O: sumun P2P me!

Skipley: Um . . .

Maximus: Rom, do you fancy me?

Throbbing_Gristle: Skip u jump out of da window . . .

Lil_Miss_Naughty: I have dat blimin u2 song in ma hed

Docman: Which 1?

[Sodgerblahboo entered the room.]

Skipley: Sorry, it wasn't me who jumped out of THE window.

Pinkfluffyhandcuffs: hi 222222222222222222uuuuuuuu-uuuuuuuu Sodger!

Throbbing_Gristle: . . . i look down & den . . . i laf again!

Lil_Miss_Naughty: da 1 dat cum out last yr

Docman: boring bean

Skipley: What exactly does that mean? Boring bean?

Throbbing_Gristle: dat wuz a pome Skip.

[R-O-M-E-O left the room.]

Maximus: wot?

Throbbing_Gristle: Skip I saw ur game n luk here nw palya da dks on u!

Skipley: Does anyone have a dictionary that I can use to translate whatever it is Throbbing_Gristle is trying to say?

Maximus: u fancy me, Skip?

Skipley: Not in this or any other lifetime, Maximus.

Lil_Miss_Naughty: time 4 me 2 say gudnite, sweet dreamz 2nite, unless u wanna bite

Docman: boring bean

Skipley: You know, that's really annoying, Docman. Does your vocabulary include any other words?

Throbbing_Gristle: u nva luved me u nva will bt evn so I luv u Skip

Sodgerblahboo stands on rooftop and sings TOON TOON BLACK & WHITE ARMY

Skipley: You are too strange for words, TG. I think you need mental help. No, seriously, don't be afraid to admit you need help.

Docman: boring bean

I left after that. It was just too idiotic. So much for a fabu chat room where peeps actually talk with each other.

So, that's pretty much my life right now—I'm going bald, I have two dates for the VB, and I'm the host to a chat room of friggin' idgets. Speaking of the VB, we're a week away from it, and surprisingly enough, it's really working! I wish I could have gotten OTP Duff on the committee, but they wouldn't let her. Something about an Obvious Teacher's Pet not being allowed to do other work in addition to prefect. I think she just got Mr. Krigon to say that because she knew I was going to stick her on the cobweb crew. Holly and Peg and Lalla and I are doing the decorations, and we get to take the second half of Friday off to decorate the gym. It's going to be *the* major coolio event of the year!

Gotta go. Term paper due next week and I have to do a gazillion footnotes and you know how long it takes to write those up. Tell me what's going on with you and Weasel Boy.

Hugs and kisses,
~Em

Subject: Fwd: Re: Details of the ghost or entity at 249 Basque Close
From: Mrs.Oded@btelecom.co.uk
To: Dru@seattlegrrl.com
Date: 24 October 2003 6:33 pm

Well, this sucks bullfrogs! Crap! Now what do I do???
Hs & Ks
~Em

Dear Miss Williams:

We at the Psychic Research Society appreciate your offer of 8 October 2003 to investigate the possible haunting of your underwear drawer, but at this time, our investigative team is booked through this year, and most of next. We will keep your request in our files, however, and should a team be in your area and have time to investigate the unusual activity with your knickers, they will contact you.

Thank you for your interest.

Best,
Ken W. Kittenshanks
PRS Vice President

Subject: I did it! Well, kind of. Almost. OK, I didn't really.
From: Mrs.Oded@btelecom.co.uk
To: Dru@seattlegrrl.com
Date: 26 October 2003 6:33 pm

Dru wrote:
> *he said that he really loved me, but that he needed*
> *his freedom. He said he felt like I was strangling*
> *him, and that he thought it would be good for us to*
> *be open to new experiences. Then he went on to*
> *say he wants to have sex, but only if Tabitha can do*
> *it with us!!!!!!!!!*

EW! Major EW! That is so sick! What a weirdo. You are so smart to dump him. You don't need him, Dru.

Your cast'll be off in another week, and then you'll be back to swimming and everything, and you know you have the hots for that senior on the guys' team, so everything will work out. I know this, and you can trust me, because I have a lot of experience with men, what with everything happening with Aidan and Devon and Fang. I know dumping V is the right thing for you, and I said all along that he was nothing but a smutmonger, and now you see that he is. So don't waste any more time thinking about it.

OK, I have some big news to tell you, but you have to sit through the dull stuff first because you always do that to me. I didn't get to write to you yesterday because we're so busy with the half-term stuff, and the big party, of course. But I wanted to tell you about the costumes—I went over to Aidan's house yesterday (which was VERY cool, let me tell you). I was really looking forward to going there and seeing him and talking about stuff, the kind of things you can't talk about in front of friends like Peg and Lalla and . . . well, *you know!* Boyfriend-and-girlfriend stuff. I guess I was hoping for something kind of like the fun that Fang and I had hanging out together after the James Bond movie, only more, if you know what I mean. Fang, he's a guy and everything, and I like him, but he's not a BF, and Aidan is, so I should get more for my money with Aidan, don't you think?

Great. Now I've confused myself. Sigh.

Back to yesterday—Devon was there, too, but he had that Pier girl with him, so Aidan and I couldn't really talk to each other like I was hoping we could.

Anyway, Aidan is wearing an über-coolio, über-fabu black leather outfit that looks very bondage-y to the ball. He's even got boots for it, and he showed me a picture of the makeup he's going to wear—it's so tight! There are three big red, bloody slash marks that go across his face, dripping blood. He's going to look abso fabso next to my white costume.

Devon and Pier left right after that, but Aidan's mom was home by then. I thought we might go up to his room so we could listen to music and talk without her rushing in every two minutes to offer us food, but he said that wasn't a good idea.

"Mum is a bit nosy when I've got birds here," he said, giving me a look so steamy it almost melted what remains of my hair (which he thinks is a stunning color, BTW). "But I really want to be with you, Emily. Now that I know you're hot, we can have a bit of fun."

I'm hot! He thinks I'm hot! Oh, I am so hot! Hey, wait a minute . . . do you think he just likes me for my body? Do you think he just wants me because I'm snogworthy? Don't get me wrong, a BF should want to snog and all, but shouldn't he love my mind, too? I love him for more than just his hottalicious bod and his fabu-coolio mustache, after all. It's the least he can do to like me for more than just the fact that I have very cool taste and know how to kiss without getting my tongue everywhere.

Still, a real girlfriend wouldn't say no to being hot, would she? "Sure, Aidan, that would be cool. Like . . . um . . . right now?"

"Oh, baby," he said, then put his hand on my hip and kind of rubbed it around. "Now is good. Look, I'll tell Mum I'm going to run you home, right?"

"OK," I said, and he jumped up and went to tell his mother he was driving me home. We got into his dad's car, and the first thing he did was grab me and kiss me! Right in the driveway! By now, of course, I am a woman of experience, so I didn't jump or anything. I just concentrated on kissing him back. His mustache tickled my lip, and he did the tongue thing, which you know I didn't really like with him (I did with Devon, though), but this time it was OK. I guess. He must have liked it, because he ground his mouth against mine and moaned a lot.

He didn't say much when he drove me toward home, just kind of gave me odd looks when I started talking about coolio bands that I like and why I think Oded is über-fabu and things like that.

Suddenly he pulled into a dark dead-end and stopped the car. Before I could say anything, he pounced on me.

"Emily, you've got me so hot," he said, kissing me again, but this time, *this time* he put his hand on my boob. Right on my boob! OK, I was wearing a tee and a sweater and my jacket, but his hand was ON MY BOOB!

"Um," I said, trying desperately to remember the rules for French kissing someone. Oh, the pressure! It's horrible! How am I expected to remember everything when a guy has his hand on my boob? What if I flunk kissing? Ack! I was back to feeling squidgy again. There I was with Aidan, who was so nummy he made my mouth water, and obviously something was wrong with me because all I could think of was that I really wished we were in his room listening to music and talking rather than sitting in a car kissing, with him groping my left boob.

I think I need a sex therapist. Maybe two, I'm sure I have some sort of monumental sex hang-up that's going to take years of therapy to straighten out.

"Mmm," Aidan said with his eyes half closed. "Touch me, duck."

"Huh?" He wanted me to touch him? THERE??? OHMIGOD!

"Come on, duck. I need you."

I melted. He needed me! Not only am I hot, he needed me! So much for all my worrying. Does it get any better than this?

Well, as it turns out, it does. At least I hope it does, because what happened next . . . Dru, I'm telling you, SOMETHING IS WRONG WITH ME! There was Aidan, kissing my lips and doing the tongue thing, and there was me, sitting all stiff and worried and feeling utterly squidgy inside.

"Come on, Em," he said, and grabbed my hand, pulling it over to him.

Only this time I didn't even let it get as far as his leg before I pulled it back.

"Well, um . . . you know, Aidan, maybe you should just take me home now." My mouth spoke before I realized what it was saying, but then the words were out and I had to act like I knew what I was talking about.

I hate that!

"What?" He stopped kissing me and frowned a little. "What do you mean I should take you home?"

"It's just that . . . um . . . I don't really want to . . . uh . . . touch you. There. Right now. Maybe another time—"

"You little tart!"

I felt awful, hurt that he called me a tart, and guilty because he needed me and I failed him, but what was I supposed to do? I didn't want to grope him, but I did want to maintain my girlfriend status. I'm willing to bet you that the evil Tash isn't afraid of a little thingie fondling. God! Why don't they have a Girlfriend 101 class to teach you how and when you're supposed to do stuff? The least they could do is make us a cheat sheet. I hate winging life like this.

I decided a little white lie wasn't going to hurt anyone. "It's not that I don't want to, it's . . . um . . . I'm not feeling so good right now. Maybe I'm coming down with a cold or something. I'm probably contagious. I think you should take me home."

I jumped back into my seat as he snarled under his breath, starting up the car and slamming his foot onto the accelerator. I was absolutely miserable. I knew I was letting him down, but Mom always said I shouldn't let any boy push me into doing things I didn't want to do. I just wished someone would tell Aidan that he wasn't supposed to get mad when I said no.

He muttered a lot on the trip home. I didn't say anything, what *could* I say, my whole life was ruined. Everything was horrible. I figured he would probably break our date for the Vamp Ball, and then he'd tell Tash that she was right all along, and I'd never have another date again because all the guys would think I was an idiot. I tried to think of something I could say to make him happy again, but my mind flaked out on me and couldn't come up with anything better than me telling Aidan my hand was sprained, and the doctor said no thingie touching for a week.

"I'd just like to know what you see in Devon."

"Devon?" Huh?

Aidan shot me an angry look. "Yes, Devon. The bloke

you were with the other night—you *do* remember the night of the party, don't you?"

OHMIGOD, you don't think he knows that I barfed all over Devon, do you? I'll die, this time I really will die. Fang said that he told Devon not to tell anyone, and Devon said he wouldn't, but what if he had? What if he told Aidan? GAH! I blinked at him a couple of times, trying to think of something to say about that night that didn't involve Devon or vomit.

"Um . . . "

"Just answer me this—are you my bird or not?"

Oh! Relationship talk! I'm much better at that than the sex stuff. "Of course I am, Aidan, if you want me to be. I mean . . . yes!"

OK, so I sounded like an idiot. Minus ten points for babbling, but plus twenty-five for not losing my cool earlier.

"Right. Then I'll be expecting you to act like it."

"Uh . . . " Do you think he was talking about sex? What if he wasn't? What if I've got it all wrong? Maybe I just have too much sex on the mind. Maybe he just wants to have a girlfriend he can talk to and go clubbing with and things like that. "Sure. So—we're going to the Vampire Ball together?"

He gave me kind of a funny look. "Right, but I expect you to be gagging for it by then."

Gagging for it? Now he really had me confused. What on earth did "gagging for it" mean? It doesn't sound like sex, does it? You don't gag when you French kiss someone, right? It must be something else. Maybe it was a funny way of saying he wanted me to be more romantic.

I worried about him all night long, but this morning I

decided that if he wants me to be his girlfriend *and* he is going to take me to the ball, that meant things are pretty coolio between us despite the thingie situation. Right? Right.

Anyway, that was yesterday. Today Holly and I went to the café. Aidan was there, without Tash (which was nice), although he didn't really pay me any attention. Devon had Pier (I guess they're a couple), and Holly sat and watched a guy at the next table, which was very intriguing. She's never shown much interest in guys, but this one, a thin black guy with a gold earring, really seemed to grab her attention. I asked her about it later, but she said she just thought he was nice to look at. Oh, sure. Like we haven't heard that one before?

Fang told me he was coming as a vampire, so I expect he'll show up in black with a cape or something. He doesn't really like the costume part of the party, I think, but it's still nice that he asked me.

Gotta run, Mom is doing yet another English dinner (steak and kidney pie, which sounds gross, but Mom took out the kidney, so it's really just a giant steak pot pie), and you know how Brother gets if we make him wait for his din-dins.

If you need to cry on my shoulder, go ahead. I might be half a world away, but I'm still here for you, girlfriend.

Lots of hugs and kisses,
~Em

Subject: Re: This is so cool!
From: Mrs.Oded@btelecom.co.uk
To: Dru@seattlegrrl.com
Date: 30 October 2003 9:40 pm

> *So I said yes, of course, and we're going to take the*
> *Spirit of Washington Dinner Train around Lake*
> *Washington on Saturday night! Isn't that just, like,*
> *mondo tight? Timothy is so different from V, much*
> *more mature, and he likes all of the same shows I*
> *like, which I think is just kismet.*

Majorly mondo tight! You have my blessing. I've known Tim McNeil since grade school, and he is a really nice guy even if he did used to pants all the girls (never me, though, because he knew I'd beat the crap out of him if he did). You'll have to tell me *everything* about how the date went. And the dinner train! That's so romantic! Oooooh!

I can't stay to write much, I've got a ton of things to do for tomorrow night. Mom took me out to a theatrical rental place today and I rented a really cool fog machine. It's going to be a surprise—I haven't told anyone about it—but everyone is going to be so friggin' impressed when the fog starts rolling out of the equipment room and fills the gym.

I think I told you we got the local bakery to do the cakes and tortes and pastries, right? They're doing the pastries in the shapes of bats—isn't that cool? In addition to them, we're having chocolate-covered strawberries, punch and coffee and tea, and some cheese-snacky things. I thought the cheese stuff ruined the layout, but Russell Crowe Krigon says that we have to have something for people who don't like chocolate. Excuse me? Who doesn't like chocolate, and do I want them at my Vampire Ball? I think not! But this country is obsessed with cheese, so cheesy crackers and stuff we have to have.

We're going to do the tables with this gorgeous dark

red crushed velvet material that one of the girls' moms gave us. We have to give it back, which is a shame, because it's really pretty, but Sam told me she'd ask her mom where she got it. As a centerpiece we'll have two huge candelabras from the theater rental place that look like they're straight out of *Dracula* (the good version, not the sucky one), cobwebs, and as a really cool touch, dried roses scattered around the table. There will be cobwebs and black gauze material on the walls, and little candles and more black gauze on the individual tables. Doesn't it sound fabulous? Oh, and we have black lights, too. I'll take tons of pictures before tomorrow night so you can see it.

Off to beddy-bye. I'm glad you're recovering so nicely. Keep your fingers crossed for me that I don't do anything else to hurt Aidan, will you? I'm starting to think I'm cursed or something.

Hugs and kisses,
~Em

P.S. My hair is a hottie magnet. Mac, one of the second-year sixth formers, asked me to the Polo Club. I told him I was busy for a bit, but maybe we could do something after the break. How tragic is it that just when I finally get really tight hair that all the guys like, it falls out? WAH!

Subject: I hope you're sitting down
From: Mrs.Oded@btelecom.co.uk
To: Dru@seattlegrrl.com
Date: 1 November 2003 10:11 am

That's a stupid subject line, of course you're sitting down! I don't know anyone who reads their e-mail standing up.

Boy, I'm pooped. I'm so tired I don't know what to feel, whether I should be looking for a rock to crawl under, or happy, or mad, or all of them. I think it's all of them, but in order to explain it, I'm going to have to start at the beginning. Otherwise it'll be too confusing.

First of all, Holly and I and the three other girls on the committee got the gym set up so it looked totally über-coolio. I had to let Holly in on my fog machine secret since it was too big for me to move by myself, so we tucked it behind a stack of mats in the equipment room. The plan was to wait until the ball started, then to push it behind the speakers for the band, and let the fog slowly trickle out across the floor. We tried it out in the equipment room, and it worked fabulously.

"You're sure this will be OK? Mr. Krigon won't be mad that you're doing this without his approval?" Holly's just not happy unless she's worrying about something.

"Of course he won't be mad. He approved everything else for the party, didn't he? And the school isn't paying for the machine, I am, so there's nothing he can complain about. Turn it so the fog is a little thicker, will you? I want to see if it hangs around the floor like it does in the movies."

She twisted a knob and the fog came out thick, and kind of lurked along the floor. I walked through it and it swam around my feet perfectly. "Oh, man, this is going to be *so* great!"

"It is very eerie," Holly said, running through it so long tendrils of fog snaked after her.

"Yeah, well, you're in charge of watching the level of

fog, OK? We'll have to have it on much higher out in the gym, since it will have to fill a much bigger space. What setting do you have it on now?"

"Three. It goes up to twelve."

"Great, it sounds like there'll be more than enough power to cover the whole floor. Okey doke, let's go out and see how the cobwebbing is going."

We got the rest of the gym decorated, turned out all of the lights except the black ones, and ran around shrieking and stuff until the janitor came in and turned the lights back on. He promised not to touch anything, so we left. Holly went to her last class, and I went home, figuring OTP Duff couldn't squeal on me, because I'd been given the half day to get ready for the party, and if getting your makeup and costume just right isn't getting ready, I don't know what is.

All right, you're dying to hear about the costume, right? Yes, there's a reason I didn't describe it to you—I wanted you to be surprised. I didn't get a picture of me in it because . . . well, I'll get to that. You'll just have to make do with a description until I get a picture.

I told you I was going as a fallen angel, in white, right? Well, the dress was white satin with a square neck, and tight sleeves to my elbows, at which point it flowed out in the medieval style. The material was really beautiful—it had this delicious white-on-white embroidery with a plain front panel (that went all the way to the floor). Attached to the back of the dress were a pair of soft, feathered wings (short ones, not the long ones) made up of that fuzzy kind of ostrich-feather stuff, not big feathers. The wings went almost to my waist. So that's the angel part of my costume. The fallen part was the black studded dog collar and matching wristbands, a long, long rope of black shiny beads that were knotted just below my boobs, and a big black crucifix that hung down to my stomach.

"What are you doing?" Bess asked as I was in the bathroom slicking back most of my hair into a bun at the nape of my neck.

I made a face at her. "What does it look like I'm doing? I'm dancing on the ceiling, of course."

"Don't be so rude," she said, sitting on the little bathroom bench. "I came in to offer my help with your makeup."

I gave her my patented Look of Utter Disbelief. "Like I *need* help with makeup?"

"You said you wanted really dramatic eyes, and I am an art major. I'll do it better than you."

I thought about that for a minute, then realized she was probably right. "OK, but if I don't like it, I'm taking it off. This is a mondo important night and I have to look just right."

"Sure. What are you doing to your bangs?"

I held up the spiking gel. "Spiking them in soft, swoopy curved spikes."

She chewed on her lip for a minute as she looked at my bangs, then jumped up. "Stay here, I've got something better."

"Something better than spiking gel?"

She came back with a small bottle in her hand and showed it to me. "It's not permanent color, it'll wash off, but I think it'll look good with your orange hair."

"It's not orange, it's Copper—"

"Sunset Splendor, I know, but that's just another name for orange. Oh, don't get all huffy on me. Just spike your bangs. This is going to look really great, and it has the added bonus of making you a walking advertisement for Halloween."

"Huh?"

"Black and orange!"

Once I got my bangs spiked she carefully applied the temporary black coloring to the ends of the spiky bits. I hate to admit that she was right, but she was. It really did look great, and very dramatic, although my hair is NOT orange.

"Now, let's see, for your eyes, I think the kohl will be best."

"I was going to use Midnight's Passion for eye shadow—"

"No, no color. Just black and white and your hair. That'll be all the color you need."

"But my lipstick—"

"Black. You have black lipstick?"

I started to nod, but she tsked and grabbed my chin, tipping my head back. "Sit still. I think an exaggerated Egyptian look is what you want."

She did my eyes, darkened my eyebrows, and then did the lipstick last. "There you go; all done. You look like an angel who's been up to all sorts of trouble."

I looked in the mirror and did a little dance. "Thanks, Bess, it's really cool."

"Told ya."

I stuck my tongue out at her and started to leave the bathroom. She grabbed my arm. "You need condoms?"

Why is everyone in this family trying to give me condoms? I mean, how many condoms can a girl use? Especially when I'm not using them? "No, I still have the last batch you gave me, and then Mom insisted on giving me some, too."

"OK, just checking; don't get your knickers in a twist."

"Oh, you are just so funny."

"Have fun, Em."

I snorted and went downstairs. Brother came out of the kitchen and did a double take at me. He turned to Mom, who was following him, and said, "You told me girls would be easier to raise than boys."

Mom smiled at him. "I lied."

I did a twirl for them, holding out my arms so the sleeves would flutter. "Well? What do you think? Do I look like a fallen angel?"

"Er . . ."

"You look very nice, dear. Doesn't she look nice?" Mom said.

"Er . . ."

"I did her makeup," Bess said, coming downstairs.

"Er . . ."

"Very striking, Bess."

"Er . . ."

I rolled my eyes and whapped Brother on the arm. "Oh, stop it! You know I look fabulous. Now come on. I have to be there early so I can show the band where to set up and stuff, and to make sure that the Old-People cheese bits are clearly segregated from all the marvy chocolate things."

Brother tried not to smile, but I saw it, and forgave him a little for not telling me how wonderful I looked. He drove me to the school and managed to include a lecture on what he called "proper behavior" but which everyone knows is just another name for being dead. Before I got out of the car, I leaned over and kissed him on the forehead. "You're really old sometimes, but you're not too bad for a father."

He looked surprised for a minute, then got a little weepy-eyed. "Thank you, Emily. Such words of praise are rare, and thus worth their weight in gold."

I smiled and got out of the car and headed into the school, feeling all warm and fuzzy. I wonder how long Mom and Bess let him wear the black lipstick kiss on his forehead?

Drat. BRB. Phone.

~Em

Subject: Back
From: Mrs.Oded@btelecom.co.uk
To: Dru@seattlegrrl.com
Date: 1 November 2003 10:46 am

Phone was Holly calling to see if I was going to kill myself or not. OK, slight exaggeration, but she did say she wondered if I was going to make Brother let me go home. I have to admit, the thought is tempting.

Back to last night. Everything started off really well. We pushed the cheese twiddles, 115 types of Stilton, cheese crackers, cheese puffs, and cheese-something with mayonnaise (the Brits put mayo on everything) that looks like what our dog used to ralph up after he'd been eating in the compost heap to one end of the table, and rearranged the rest (chocolate, chocolate, chocolate) to display at maximum coolness.

I had told Fang and Aidan that I had to be at the gym early (which allowed me to avoid the problem of who got to pick me up), but I was watching for them both.

"You're going to stick like glue to me, right?" I asked Holly.

"Right."

"And if I do this?" I made a circular signal with my left hand.

"Erm . . . left hand, distract Aidan."

"And this?" I did a zigzag with my right.

"Dance with Fang?"

"Right. And what about this?" I grinned really wide and made a backward-and-forward motion with my forefinger.

"Uh . . . "

"Do I have any lipstick on my teeth?"

"Oh, that's right, that's the teeth check signal. Sorry. I won't forget again."

I patted her on the shoulder. "Just relax and have fun."

"Relax!" She heaved a really big sigh. "I'm supposed to dance with both Aidan and Fang! How can I relax?"

"Oh, come on, you've known them for two months—they're just guys! They won't bite." She nodded and gave me a relieved smile. I thought about Devon nibbling my neck. "Well, maybe they would, but they'd ask first. I'm pretty sure they'd ask."

She was back to looking worried, so I set her on door watch so she could let me know the minute either date arrived. It would have been easier if she'd had a date, too, but no one asked her, and she's too shy to ask a guy, and when I asked her if she wanted me to see if I couldn't get one of the fifth form guys to ask her, she had an asthma attack and had to go sit in the office until she could breathe again.

Devon was the first of the three guys to arrive. He came alone, which surprised me. I had told him he could come to the ball as long as he didn't bring a date, figuring no one would know he wasn't a sixth form student as long as he wore a costume, but I didn't actually expect him to do as I asked. He's such a flirt, I figured it was impossible for him to come to a party alone. I was wrong. He walked in the door, flipped off a long dark green cape, and turned to face me.

Holly ran toward me, her eyes huge. "Did you see? Devon's here and he's dressed as a knight!"

"Hoo!" I blew out a breath and just about ate Devon up with my eyes. He was SO UTTERLY FABU! He had on black leggings, boots that cross-gartered up his legs (I'm not Brother's daughter for nothing), a dark green hauberk, chain mail that reached to his knees, and a broadsword belted at his side. He was almost as scrummy as that Viggo guy in *Lord of the Rings*. "Holy cow, he's gorgeous!"

"You don't expect me to dance with him, do you?" Holly asked, kind of panicky.

"You mean in place of me? Not on your life! If I weren't so madly in love with Aidan, I'd try to snag Devon. As it is, he's going to have to ask me to dance at least once, or I'll die."

Just then Devon saw us and smiled, which made something inside me melt, then I melted even more when he came over to where Holly and I were clinging to each other. I pried her cold fingers off my wrist and struck a cool *I'm not slobbering over you* pose. Or I tried to—I'm not absolutely sure I was successful, because Devon's smile got bigger the closer he came.

"My angel! How wonderful you look. Positively dripping with all sorts of delicious sins. And Holly—what a charming elf you make."

"I'm a water sprite," she whispered, her eyes still huge

as she looked him over. You know, Dru, I've never understood Brother's fascination with medieval stuff, but if this is what those knights looked like, I'm going to have to rethink my policy of avoiding everything Middle Ages.

"You look great, Devon. That's a fabulous costume."

"Had it made up last year when Mum was into the Ren Faire scene. Now, you told me you want me to mingle, but before I do, you have to promise to dance with me. Both of you," he said politely, and I did a little swoon inside. If only I weren't so madly in love with Aidan . . .

"Sure," I said quickly, then pinched Holly until she gasped out something that sounded like a yes.

"Wow," I said, watching him as he strolled off, one hand on his sword. "He's really something, isn't he?"

"Aidan's here," Holly said, pulling me toward the door. "At least, I think it's him."

I looked. Although I'd seen a picture of what Aidan's makeup was going to look like, I had to admit that seeing it in person was really wild. He'd whited out his face a bit, then painted on three long slash marks that went from above his eyebrows down across his nose and cheek. It was *really* cool.

"Hi, Aidan," I said as I hurried over to him. "That makeup is fabu."

"Should be, took long enough to get it right. You look good."

I opened my mouth to say that the rest of his costume was wonderful as well, but he grabbed me and hauled me up and stuck his tongue in my mouth! I mean, he kissed me, but his tongue was right there. I didn't know what to do, I really didn't. On the one hand, it was über-cool to be kissed like that in front of everyone, but on the other hand, I really didn't like the way he was doing it, kind of like he had the right to just grab me and stick his tongue in my mouth whenever he wanted to, kind of like I had no say in the whole thing, which is stupid, because it was MY mouth.

I decided I didn't like it, and pushed back until he retrieved the tongue-o-matic.

"What's this, being a tease again?" he asked in a snotty voice.

I just stared at him. It was awful, Dru! Here was the guy I've been crazy about for the last two months, and it was our big night, and he was horrible to me! "No, I'm not a tease. I just don't like being mauled."

He smiled then, but I have to say, it wasn't a very nice smile. It was more of a sneer. "That's not what I hear."

I had this sick feeling in my stomach and suddenly wanted to go home, but I couldn't because A) it was my party, and B) I am not a kid anymore and I can't give in to the sick-stomach feeling, and besides, I don't like it when people sneer at me. "Maybe you ought to get your ears cleaned, then. I'm going to go over there and talk to some people who don't want to stick their tongue in my mouth."

"Emily," he said as I left, but I ignored him, more than a little bit miffed, but at the same time feeling rotten because everything I'd planned to happen with Aidan seemed to be going wrong and I didn't know why.

"I hate this," I told Holly a few minutes later. "I hate feeling like this. I'm going to go talk to Aidan and ask him what's wrong."

"You can't," she said, then pointed. "Fang is here."

"Where? Holy cow! What happened to him and

Devon? Did they drink some sort of hottie potion or something?"

Fang stood near the door being greeted by a guy done up in black with huge horns curling back off his head, but I ignored him to give Fang the eye. He was dressed in one of those frilly-front shirts with lace in place of cuffs, a black, really tight-fitting short coat like they wear in those movies with guys from the Victorian era, and a scarlet vest thingy. His hair was tied back in a teeny, tiny ponytail. Fang doesn't really have hair that's long, but he managed to get a little ponytail that looked *so cool* with the rest of the outfit. He looked . . . *elegant*. It was so un-Fang-like, I couldn't help but stare.

"Man, if this is what happens when they go to a costume party, we're going to have to start having them every month!"

Holly snickered.

We went over to say hi. Fang told Holly she looked nice, then he turned to me, walked all the way around me, then stopped in front and tipped his head to one side. "That suits you."

"What does? The crucifix? The black and Copper Sunset Splendor? The medieval gown with fwoofy sleeves?"

"The wings. You look like an angel." He took my hand and turned it over, then he kissed my palm.

I almost melted on the spot! It was so romantic! I mean, there was Fang looking just as marvelous as Devon, only in a completely different way, and he kissed my palm. I went all melty. It made me realize how much more I *didn't* like Aidan shoving his tongue into my mouth.

"Thank you," I said, then decided what the heck, so I

turned my hand around in his, and kissed his palm. Holly made kind of a gasping noise behind me, but I didn't care. I was busy enjoying the look of surprise in Fang's eyes.

"Why did you do that?" he asked, his eyebrows (two, no hint of Unibrow) smooshing together.

I have no idea why I did it, but I wasn't going to tell him that. There is a limit to how stupid I'm willing to appear. "Same reason you did."

Holly eeked.

Fang's eyebrows de-smooshed. "I doubt that."

Holly grabbed my arm.

"Just a second, Holly. Really, Fang? Why did you—"

"There you are. Fancy dress suits you, mate, you look like something out of Jane Austen. Maybe you should stop grubbing around vet school and go apply at the BBC. Bet they'd snap you up. Doesn't my little Emily look stunning sexy tonight?" Aidan came up and put his arm around me, pulling me up next to him.

Oh, crap!

"Your little Emily?" Fang cocked an eyebrow at Aidan.

"Jealous? You needn't be, old man, there's enough birds to go around. Just keep your hands off mine."

OHMIGOD! Jealous? Fang? Of Aidan? I looked at Fang. He didn't look jealous, but he didn't look happy, either. To be honest, he looked kind of sad, like I had hurt him.

He glanced at Aidan, then back to me. I just stood there like a total and complete idiot, unable to say anything. "I see. You always were a lucky sod, Aidan. I hope you appreciate what you've got this time." Then he gave me a little nod and turned to Holly and asked her if she wanted to dance. I stared after them, my heart sort of crumpling up into a painful ball.

I had made Fang feel bad.

Aidan started snogging my neck as they went off to dance, murmuring, "Don't mind him, duck, he's just a bit green because I've got the bit of goods tonight."

It was all my fault—I made Fang feel bad. No, it was Aidan's fault, too. He made *me* feel bad. "Bit of goods? BIT OF GOODS? So first I'm a tease, and now I'm a *bit of goods?*"

What sort of a horrible person makes someone as nice as Fang feel bad? I looked at Aidan, really looked at him. He just laughed and pulled me toward the dance area, making sure to rub his crotch against me. "Don't be such a twit, Emily. Let's dance."

Why hadn't I ever noticed that his eyes were so hard? Why hadn't I realized that I had stopped being in love with him, and just thought I was? Why hadn't I seen through his hottie face and mustache and body and figured out that being with him always made me unhappy? No one else did. Just him.

And now he had made me hurt Fang's feelings.

"Don't want to dance?" he breathed into my ear, his 'stache tickling me. "I can think of something else for us to do, something perfect for my luscious little fallen angel."

I jerked my hand away from him and pushed him back. "I've changed my mind. I'm undating you. You are no longer my date for tonight, so that means you can't haul me around like I was a sack of potatoes."

"Emily—"

I jerked away when he tried to grab me, and raised my voice a bit, just so he could hear me over the music. "And you can't stick your tongue in my mouth unless you ask first, got that? It's only polite!"

"Emily—" he said again, only this time he kind of growled it.

"And you can't make Fang look sad anymore. I don't like it," I said a bit louder. Yeah, I was really losing my temper, but boy, if anyone had it coming, he did.

"Will you stop—"

"You're not a very nice person, Aidan. I don't like you anymore!" A couple of people around us turned to look.

"For Christ's sake, you slag-faced cow, *shut up!*" he yelled.

"And you know what else? I don't want to touch your thingie, so you can just stop asking me to!" I yelled right back at him.

OK, so maybe I shouldn't have yelled that, but it probably would have been OK if the music hadn't stopped right then, and my words echoed off the gym walls so everyone could hear them.

I stood and stared in horror at him for a minute as the echo of me saying I didn't want to touch his thingie rattled around the room, then I tried really hard to faint, but you know how it is—just when you want to faint, you can't. I looked around. Everyone was standing perfectly still, staring at us.

"Stupid little slut," Aidan hissed at me. "No bit of pussy is worth this!"

I could see Mr. Krigon (dressed in a cape and wearing fake vamp teeth with bits of blood dribbling from the corners of his mouth) walking very fast toward us, so I didn't say anything else to Aidan, even though I wanted to tell him that he was the biggest poop I'd ever met. Instead I turned around and headed toward the equipment room. I figured I'd turn on the fog machine, then have a good cry in there for a bit.

"Emily!"

"Sorry, Mr. Krigon, I'm just going to turn on the fog machine."

"Fog machine? What fog machine? Emily—"

I pushed my way through the crowd in the dance area, past Snickerer Ann (tight red dress that showed she had no boobs, and long black wig) and Snickerer Bee (dressed like a shepherdess, of all things), both of whom laughed really loudly when I passed them, past Mrs. Spreadborough (pumpkin, complete with little green vine hat) who looked shocked, past Miss Horseface (not wearing any costume) who flared her equine nostrils as I ran by, past Devon, who was leaning up against the wall, laughing (no doubt at me), past a horrified Holly standing really close to Fang, who watched me with an odd look on his face, past everyone else who ignored the fact that the band had started playing, and watched me run by instead. Me, the fool American who hurt a really nice guy because of a horrible one.

I bit my lip hard, refusing to let them see me cry. I hated them all, hated England, hated Brother for making me come here, and most of all, hated myself for being so stupid about Aidan the Poophead.

I ran into the equipment room and flipped the fog machine on, then cranked it up so it thumped and hummed loudly as it belched fog out of the end of the long hose that snaked around to the edges of the band's amps. No one out there deserved nice, eerie fog, but I was going to show them that I wasn't bothered by a little thing like the whole world hearing that I didn't want to touch Aidan's thingie. I'd just stay in the equipment room for a bit, then go out and act like nothing happened, and then I'd go home and die.

You have to admit it was the only thing I could do.

"Emily?" Holly stood in the door, Fang behind her. "Are you all right?"

"Fine and friggin' dandy." I sniffled, turning around so she wouldn't see me wiping up my tears. I knew I'd ruined my really cool makeup, but at that moment I honestly didn't care, which should tell you just how upset I was. I mean, have you ever known me to slack off in the makeup department?

"Are you going to come out?"

"Yeah, in a few minutes. I'm just making sure the machine is working OK."

"Oh. All right. I'll see you when you come out."

"Sure," I said, still facing the wall.

There was silence for a few seconds, and when I glanced back, Holly was still standing in the doorway. "I . . . I'm sorry, Emily."

"I know. Thanks."

She left quietly, and I felt even worse. I thought maybe Fang would have said something nice to me, but he didn't. He didn't say anything, he just stood behind Holly, and left when she left. Obviously he didn't want anything more to do with me. My heart broke up into even smaller pieces. I cried for a lot longer, but after a while I decided that although my life was now formally over, I wasn't so pathetic that I was going to hide away for the rest of the evening.

"This is my party, dammit. I worked hard to make it the absolute coolest thing this stupid school has ever seen, and I'm not going to let some poophead make me sit in here and hide from him."

"Emily?" It sounded like Mr. Krigon calling for me. I sighed. The fog machine gave a gurgle and continued to thump and hum away.

"Emily? Where are you? Emily, this—Oh, I beg your pardon. Yes, I'm very sorry, I'm trying to stop it. Emily?"

I took a deep breath, tried to make my stomach stop thinking it was going to barf, then pushed the door open to go back into the gym.

There was no gym to be seen. Everything was sucked up into a wall of whiteness.

"Wow, that fog machine really works," I said, peering through the white to see dark shapes flit back and forth. "Guess I turned it on a bit too high."

"Emily?" Mr. Krigon called. I couldn't see him, but he sounded fairly close by. "Emily turn the machine—"

Just then the fire sprinklers went off. Mr. Krigon said later that they were very sensitive ever since the school had a fire the year before, but I say that fake fog shouldn't have set them off no matter how sensitive they were. Evidently I was wrong, though, because they went off, dumping water on everyone. The guys in the band started yelling and throwing stuff over their amps and guitars, Mr. Krigon was yelling for me to turn the damned machine off, and everyone else yelled and ran around in the fog trying to find a way out of the gym.

By the time I turned off the machine and ran back to the gym, someone had found the doors and thrown them open. Fog rolled out the door, twisted and torn by bodies as everyone raced through it to get out of the indoor downpour.

I ran across the floor, too, slipping and sliding on the heels of the last of the crowd, my dress soaked, my cute little fluffy white wings sodden, and as I found out later, my black eye makeup streaked down my cheeks all the way to my jaw. As I came through the door, I stopped. I didn't want to stop, but I had to. Everyone was standing outside, wet, teeth chattering, hair dripping, and all of them, every single one of them had turned to face me as I came out the door. OK, "glare" would be a better word. They all GLARED at me.

"Um . . . " I swallowed hard and decided I was too mortified to cry. I couldn't even summon up a prayer for instant death. "I think there was a little problem with the fog machine."

Have you ever heard a crowd growl? It's not pleasant. In fact, it kind of scared the crap out of me.

"Sorry, everyone."

They growled even louder, then Mr. Pilot, the janitor, came up behind me. "I've turned the bleedin' sprinklers off, but there's a hell of a mess to be cleaned up, not to mention three coats of my best varnish ruined."

Mr. Krigon, who was standing in front of me, sighed, his shoulders slumping as he looked at me, then he shook his head and walked past without saying anything.

Honestly, I would have felt better if they'd stoned me or put me on the pillory or whatever other torture they do in this country. All of the teachers filed past me, none of them saying anything, but all of them giving me the same look.

"Sorry," I told the fifth and sixth form kids who stood around wet, most of their costumes ruined, shivering in the cold. "It was an accident."

None of them said anything to me, either. Not directly, although a lot of them muttered stuff that made me flinch. Some of them left, others went back into the gym until the only three people left standing on the steps were me, Holly, and Aidan.

Aidan looked at me like I was a booger he'd found in his sandwich. "Bloody brilliant, Emily. Bloody brilliant." He stopped next to me and gave me a smile that didn't reach his eyes. "I thought after Dev screwed your brains out that you might be worth my time, but I was wrong."

"What?" I asked. "What are you talking about? I've never had sex with Devon."

"Oh, get off it. We all know you spent the night in Dev's bed after his party. I saw you going off with him, and I know Dev—there's no way he'd get a bird in his room and not screw her silly."

I lifted my chin, wondering why I ever thought he was so scrumptious. He was just a slimeball, really. I guess maybe it was the accent that threw me, because normally I'm pretty good at spotting slimeballs. "I didn't spend the night in his room. Fang took me home."

He snorted. "That's your story. Tash was right—you *are* a stupid little bint who doesn't know her arse from her elbow."

"You know what's wrong with your costume, Aidan?" I asked.

He squinted his eyes at me and sneered again. "Nothing?"

"Nope. It's the blood. It's fake."

He blinked at me.

"What it needs is real blood." I smiled at him, made a fist the way Bess had shown me after she took a self-defense class, and punched him as hard as I could in the nose. He screamed and fell backward through the door. Holly stood at the end of the stairs, her hands gripping the metal railing, her mouth an O of surprise as I rubbed my sore knuckles.

"I think I'm going to go home and die now. Are you OK to get home?" She nodded. "All right. Don't stand out in the cold too long, you'll get pneumonia or something. Sorry I got your sprite costume wet."

I headed off toward the road, then decided that as long as the entire school hated me, I might as well compound my sins, and walked across the front lawn that students were strictly forbidden to walk across.

"Emily!"

Someone called my name behind me. Someone male. I ignored him.

"Emily, wait."

I walked even faster. I was shaking with cold, and nerves, and my stomach was churning, but I felt really good about punching the Poopy Slimeball's nose. I hoped I gave him a nosebleed. Or broke his nose. That would be cool, too.

"Emily, stop!"

That was a second voice. I stopped and looked back. Fang and Devon were running toward me, Devon holding the cape I'd worn over my costume, Fang with one of the emergency gym blankets under his arm.

"Fang, you remember when I barfed on Devon and you took me home and I said I couldn't ever see you again because I would die of embarrassment? Well, this is a hundred times worse, so if you don't want me to curl up and die right here, don't come any closer."

Devon laughed and punched Fang in the arm. "Don't be stupid. If I had a pound for every time I tossed my cookies on someone, I'd be a rich man."

"You *are* a rich man," Fang told him as they stopped

in front of me, then he punched Devon in the arm, too.

"Why are you doing that?" I asked, momentarily distracted from my horrible, ghastly, depressing, miserable existence to wonder why they were punching each other.

"Fang and I had a little bet." Devon smiled, and put my cape around my shoulders. "I bet him that this party wouldn't go off without some sort of disaster, and he bet me that the disaster would be you finding out the truth about Aidan."

Fang put the blanket around me as well. I looked between them, then punched Devon in the arm. It hurt a lot worse than Aidan's nose because of the chain mail, but I just rubbed my knuckles and glared at him. "Why did you tell him I slept with you?"

Devon's smile melted. "I didn't. I wouldn't tell him that, Emily. It's just . . . well, I have a bit of a reputation, and he didn't see you go home, so he assumed . . . "

"You could have told him that we didn't do anything!"

"I did. He didn't believe me."

I turned to Fang and thought about punching him in the arm, too, but my knuckles were too sore. So I pinched him. Hard.

"Ow!"

"You could have told me what was going on! You could have warned me! Aidan is your friend."

"I didn't know until tonight. I've been busy at the stables and with my classes." He tipped his head to the side and looked at me. "Would you have believed me if I had known and said anything?"

I clutched my blanket and the cape tight across my chest. "I don't know." Fang's sad brown eyes made me admit the truth. "OK, I do know. I probably wouldn't have listened."

"We told you he was a mixer."

"Oh, right, so all of this is my fault?"

"Some of it, yes," Fang said.

I was just on the verge of a pout when I admitted to myself he was right.

Devon threw his arm around me, turning me around so we were headed back toward the school. Fang walked along on my other side.

"I'm not going back in there, Devon. I'm never going to be able to go back again. I'll have to go to a different school."

Devon squeezed my shoulders. "We're not going back in."

"Then where are we going?"

"Fang and I are going to take you home. My car is parked over this way."

"Good. I'd die if I had to see any of them again."

"Don't let it bother you. Dev did the same thing at our school," Fang said, reaching under the blankets to hold my hand. His fingers were nice and warm, and I have to admit it was kind of nice walking with the two of them. I wished Holly could see me.

"Really? You set the sprinklers off during a party?"

"Not during a party, during the awards ceremony at the end of the year. I was in the fifth form, and having a smoke behind a screen, and next thing I knew, the sprinklers went off and soaked everyone, kids, parents, teachers. It was a right bungle. My mum still talks about it."

"Oh." That made me feel a little bit better, but not much. "Did you quit that school because you couldn't face anyone ever again?"

Devon's arm jiggled when he laughed. "Not likely. I became the hero of the school after that. Some of my mates offered me money to do it again, just for a lark."

"Yeah, but I ruined a party! That's a hundred times worse than ruining an awards ceremony."

"It'll go down in Gob-botty history as the party to have been at, just you see," Fang said.

A little tiny bit of hope started to grow inside me. "You really think so?"

"I know so."

We were in front of Devon's car by then. Fang held the door open, and I scooted into the back. "What about Aidan? I . . . um . . . punched him in the nose."

Devon and Fang grinned at each other.

"We know. Aid came in spurting blood, yelling about you attacking him. Fang figured you'd want a ride home, so we set out to find you. Holly told us where you went."

"I'm not sorry I did it. I know he's your friend and all, but he really had it coming."

"Don't worry about it, Emily," Fang said. "We'll have a thing or two to say to him, as well."

I sat back and let myself relax a little. This was kind of nice, like having two real knights protecting my honor, except I never bought into that whole thing with a woman having to be saved by a man. I mean, we are the superior sex; we can save ourselves. Still, sometimes it's nice to have friends by your side. "Really? You mean like you're going to beat him up because he called me a bint?"

"Well, maybe not beat him up, but we'll be having a few words with the laddie," Devon said.

"Oh." I thought about that for a bit. "OK. That works for me. Would you tell him something for me?"

Devon smiled at me in the rearview mirror. "Anything you like."

"Would you tell him I've got a pair of big shoes my friend Dru calls ballbusters, and if he spreads any rumors about me, I'll show him how they got that name?"

Both Fang and Devon laughed, and I felt much better, even though my life was utterly and completely ruined.

So that was my big party. I'm going to go take a nap now. I just can't think about this anymore.

Hugs and kisses,
~Em

Subject: Re: The party they'll always remember
From: Mrs.Oded@btelecom.co.uk
To: Dru@seattlegrrl.com
Date: 3 November 2003 8:40 am

Dru wrote:
> stop worrying about it, OK? People are going to
> think you're the coolest thing ever. Honest. Stuff like
> that happens all the time to you, and you always
> survive. You just have to look at what's good and
> ignore the rest. I ignore bad stuff all the time!

Fang swears to me that everyone will think that the party was the best one ever thrown, not because it was so fabulous, but because it was so awful. That kind of makes sense, doesn't it? I mean, think of grunge—it's so horrible that everyone loves it. So I'm hoping that maybe you're both right.

Holly said she heard from a couple of girls how much fun they had despite the sprinklers, so . . . well, I've thought about it for a bit. There's bound to be a lot more to put up with from the teachers and the

Snickerers, but you're right about the good stuff. I mean, Devon and Fang really are sweet, and both looked so hot at the party, and neither of them was pissed that their costumes got wet or that they had to leave the party early. Also, both kind of defended me to Aidan, which is very cool.

You help, too, with all your advice and just being there and stuff. It's funny, isn't it, how I was telling you to dump Vance, when all along I should have dumped Aidan. Life is weird that way, huh?

So I guess I'll stay. I've just got one more month of school once the term starts back up, then I get to go do Work Experience in Scotland in January, so I won't be at school at all then. Yes, I'll have to deal with Aidan, but there's Holly and Fang and Devon and Peg and Lalla to give me sanity. Bess promised to take Holly and me to see *Stomp* and the Hard Rock Café in London, and Mom said she's going to take me to a hair doctor to see if there's anything that can stop me from going bald. Plus, Holly's mom knows a real psychic, so I'm going to have her hold a séance in my room to contact the spirit of my underwear drawer. That should be mondo cool, and I'm really looking forward to getting my drawer back. I'll let you know how that turns out.

Brother even said this morning that I might be able to go to Paris for a couple of weeks next spring in order to improve my French, so all in all, I guess it won't be too horrible to stay here.

I mean, it's not like anything worse can happen to me, right?

Hugs and kisses,
~Em

Katie Maxwell is a dyed-in-the-wool Anglophile who spent a deliriously happy year working in Harrods, a very prestigious department store in London. An eclectic reading taste covering everything from her beloved blue tweed Nancy Drews to two-hundred-year-old newspapers and magazines have given her a taste for the absurd, eccentric, and downright wacky. Katie studied physics and astronomy at the University of Washington, but decided that creating her own little worlds was much more fun than debating the existence of a black hole at the center of the Milky Way. She spends her days amusing her husband and dogs, tormenting her Sims, and hanging around online. Katie also writes adult romances under the name of Katie MacAlister. If you'd like to drop her a line, you can visit her website at www.katiemaxwell.com, or send snail mail to:

Katie Maxwell
c/o Three Seas Literary Agency
PO Box 8571
Madison, WI 53708

SMOOCH believes in helping everyone find her inner glam girl, so we've teamed up with JANE cosmetics to help make it even easier. (See opposite page.)

For more "fabu" offers, including free books and makeup, visit <u>www.smoochya.com</u>.